Piña Colada Calamity

Tanya Westlake

Impractical Press

Chapter One

"Good morning, listener! This is WBUZ, The Buzz. You're caller number thirteen, and you are *on the air*! If you know the answer to today's trivia question, you could be our weekly winner!"

"Hi, I'm—"

"This has been a tough question, and two callers have already missed it. Do you know the answer?"

"Yes, I think—"

"I can't believe no one's gotten it yet, and—"

"George, shut up and let the lady answer."

"Right, right. Caller, go ahead."

"I'm shoving a sock in George's mouth so you can get a word in, sweetie," the radio show's co-host announced with a laugh.

"Hi Celeste! I'm a big fan of your show. And I think I have the answer."

"Great, go ahead, honey."

"*Is it 'Your Tentative Love' by the Freudian Slips?*"

Celeste, the co-host, laughed out loud. "You owe me twenty bucks, George!"

1

"I can't believe anyone remembers that song! What's your name, love?" the host sounded genuinely impressed.

"Tess Russo."

"Well, Tess Russo, you have just won today's challenge, and if you can guess this week's magic number, the grand prize is all yours."

Tess looked at her cheat sheet and saw that four, seven, and three had already been tried by previous contestants that week.

"Uh, two?"

There was silence for a moment, and then the co-host screamed, "*Yes!!* Queen Tess, mistress of random music trivia and the luckiest girl in town." She started laughing hysterically, and George had to take over.

"Tess Russo, you have just won a seven-night cruise for two to the Western Caribbean! That includes full accommodations, complimentary spa treatments, and stops in beautiful Cozumel, Montego Bay, and Grand–"

But Tess was too busy jumping up and down and screaming to listen. She needed a vacation like no one else in the history of the world, and right now she needed to call Kallie Brooks, her best friend, to let her know they were going on a *cruise!*

"I'm pretty sure there's a free bar on that ship, George," Celeste chirped.

"Then we might be joining you, Tess Russo!"

"Thank you! Thank you *so* much!" Tess yelled back to them, barely containing her happy tears.

* * * * *

Six months ago, Kalliope Brooks would have been asleep at this time of the morning, having worked on the night shift for the past six years at the Lazy Gecko. But after a murder at the bar, which had gotten a little too close for comfort, her boss had forced her to switch to the day shift. Surprisingly, she was loving it, and today she'd been cooking breakfast while her father read to her from the newspaper – until the phone rang.

"Hey Kal, guess what?" her best friend Tess immediately asked on the phone.

Kallie wasn't much of a guesser, but knowing Tess and the breathless tone of her voice, it had to be good. "You're outside my door with a spinach quiche?" she replied jokingly.

"Nope."

"With a spinach quiche and home fries?"

"Better!"

"A spinach quiche, home fries, and a replacement rear view mirror for my car?" she added with a laugh.

Kallie's old but reliable car had a lot of missing

and broken parts, but she knew Tess wasn't crazy enough to start searching for scrapyard auto parts. She was just teasing her friend to get to the point.

"I won us a cruise!"

"WHAT?"

"I just won a cruise on WBUZ, like ten minutes ago. We're going to the land of palm trees and fruity umbrella drinks! Well, we already live in the land of palm trees and fruity umbrella drinks, technically. But one where we don't have to work and cabana boys bring us fluffy towels and suntan lotion."

"Tess, are you kidding me?"

"No! I'm coming over right now, and I'll show you the email from the radio station. We're going on *vacation*!"

* * * * *

Tess showed up at the door half an hour later with the printed email in her hand and a grin bigger than the whole state of Florida.

Kallie's dad opened the door and happily hugged her. "Both of you need a vacation, Tess! Promise to drink a piña colada for me!"

"You got it, Mister B!"

Sherman, Kallie's border collie mix rescue dog, danced around their feet, unsure of why everyone was so happy but glad to join in.

"Okay, let's see it," Kallie called from the kitchen, where she was loading the dishwasher after breakfast.

They all went to the dining room table to read the fabulous email, and turned on WBUZ just for good measure.

"Oh my gosh," Kallie breathed happily. She read the email out loud, "The contestant has won a seven-night, eight-day cruise for two on HappySail Cruise Lines, without exchange rights except in case of weather emergency. It's not romantic, but it sounds *legal*!"

"Look, they're paying for other stuff, too," Kallie's dad added, putting on his glasses and pointing at the fine print. "This says it's all-inclusive."

Tess and Kallie yelped and hugged and possibly cried a little. They'd both had a tough year.

"Dad, are you okay with keeping Sherman?" Kallie asked.

"Of course, kiddo. We'll have a blast, and I'll send pictures and videos every day. He likes Anna more than me, anyway. As long as she comes by to visit, he'll be as happy as a clam in sand."

Anna was Benny Brooks's new girlfriend, a lovely lady who lived down the street, and Sherman liked her as much as Benny and Kallie did. If not more.

Kallie thanked him profusely and then started to worry about the details. She'd need clothes, and someone to cover her shifts at work, and money for the bills, and what about putting on a *bathing suit*?!

Tess could apparently see her best friend steaming up, because she quickly yanked her out of it.

"You can stress about the details later, Kal. Let's go buy some big, floppy straw hats for the trip!"

* * * * *

In the six years that she'd been working at the Lazy Gecko, Kallie had certainly taken her share of unpaid days off, but never a whole week. She knew she'd need to discuss it with her boss and close friend, Marcy. When she got to work that day at ten a.m., Kallie went straight to the office to speak with her.

"Hey Marcy, I have a question for you," Kallie called, leaning into the office doorway.

Marcy looked up from her shopping list of items for the bar and smiled. "Sure, come sit down. What's up?"

Sitting down in the rolling office chair, Kallie started to explain awkwardly, "So Tess had a surprise for me this morning. She won some contest on the radio, and the prize was a week-long cruise."

"Kallie, that's amazing!" Marcy replied with a

grin.

"She wants me to go with her..."

Marcy snorted a laugh. "Well, *obviously*! You two are joined at the hip; who else would she take?"

"Is it okay if I go?"

"Are you kidding? Of course you can go! When have you ever taken more than two days off in a row? If you broke your leg, you'd be back at work before the plaster on your cast finished drying."

Kallie blushed, knowing it was true.

"You need some time off, anyway," Marcy added with a concerned frown. "I asked Mike to convince you to take some time off after–" She waved her hand vaguely, to avoid mentioning the recent murder. "I'm glad you're finally doing it."

Relieved at Marcy's answer, Kallie added, "Do I need to find someone to cover me? It's a whole week."

"Actually, I already have the perfect person in mind," Marcy answered, pointing at Kallie with her pen and winking. "Isabel wants Carlos to switch to the day shift."

"Oh, but Carlos isn't a bartender."

"He was! When I hired him nine years ago, he started off as a *great* bartender," Marcy said. "But even at that young age, he was so professional and good with people, I switched him to manager after about a year. He won't have any trouble covering for you, and it'll give him a chance to see if the day shift works for him."

Kallie nodded agreeably, glad to be helping her friend in the process. "Isabel told me her mom is taking care of the baby during the day, so she can get back to work at her yoga studio. That'll be perfect; they can both be home in the evenings together. He's such an awesome dad."

"They'll probably drive each other crazy for the first week, since he's been managing the night shift for so long, but it'll be better in the end." Marcy looked around to make sure they were alone before confiding, "I'm going to make Mike the new night manager if it all works out, but don't tell him."

"He'll be great as a manager! I won't tell him, I promise." Kallie had been friends with Mike for years, and he was practically like a brother to her.

"So go on your trip and have fun," Marcy concluded, standing up from her desk to walk out with Kallie. "The Lazy Gecko will still be standing when you get back. But I hate to think of all the trouble you two will get into!"

"I promise not to call you for bail money from Cozumel," Kallie joked. She and Tess were as silly as two monkeys in a tuxedo, but they were mostly harmless.

* * * * *

"So I hear Tess won a prize on the radio," Kallie's friend, Detective Morrison, mentioned with a smile the next morning, biting into a strip of bacon. They met for breakfast in this little outdoor café a few times every month, always early in the mornings before it got too hot, and too crowded.

"*What?!* How did you hear about that already? It was only two days ago."

"A guy I work with was listening to the radio when it happened, actually. He was on the way to work, and he told me because–"

"Yes?" Kallie asked with a grin, her glass of iced coffee poised in midair.

"I may have mentioned the two of you – occasionally – around the station."

"I see," Kallie replied with a knowing nod. "And did this 'mentioning' involve a lot of swearing?"

"Actually, now that you mention it–" Morrison mused.

"And throwing things? And very loudly wishing we'd mind our own business and stop trying to get ourselves killed?"

"Were you secretly eavesdropping on the police station, Kallie?" Her friend stared at her, pretending shock. "Because that's a *suspiciously* accurate description."

Kallie laughed out loud and cut a bite-sized

chunk from her blueberry pancakes. A waitress refilled their water glasses, smiling at their friendly early-morning banter.

"So now you're going to drive a handful of Caribbean and Mexican local governments insane, instead of just the lowly St. Petersburg police?" he continued.

"Well, you know a girl has to raise her standards, Morrison. You can't be the *only* one tearing your hair out over our shenanigans."

"Shenanigans," he repeated, pausing to consider, and then pointing at her with a strip of bacon. "That seems like a slight understatement, but I'll let it slide. So I'm not going to be getting any calls about you tripping over a dead body?"

"I promise," Kallie answered sincerely.

Morrison raised an eyebrow. "I don't want to be forced to tell any detectives in Cozumel or Grand Cayman to lock you in your room, for their own safety."

Kallie squinted at him suspiciously. "I think you do."

"Maybe a little," Morrison agreed. "But I'm glad you're finally taking a vacation, so maybe they could just put you in an ankle monitor."

"Oh, that's very generous of you, thanks," Kallie replied with a smile, sipping her orange juice.

Kallie rarely saw Carlos at work anymore, since they were on separate shifts – so she quite often dropped in to see his little family at home.

"He hates it when I watch him draw," Isabel whispered to Kallie as they curled up on a tiny couch in the corner of Studio Alvarez. The sun was setting, and it cast a swirl of color over the mostly black and white artwork.

"But you do it anyway?" Kallie asked, grabbing playfully at their baby's toes, to her delight.

"Of course. It's a wife's prerogative to be annoying, right?" She laughed.

"Hello?" Carlos interrupted, waving his charcoal-tinted hands. "I'm right here?"

"I still can't believe you held out on me all those years, Carlos. Never telling me you were such a great artist."

"He's so shy about it, Kallie," Isabel explained. "Even I wouldn't have known, if I hadn't caught him sketching during a call with my parents."

The shape of a snowy egret took form on the huge canvas, as Carlos continued drawing. Since the bird was almost entirely white, Kallie was fascinated to see how it mostly appeared as a gap in the dark background. He didn't even use a photo, drawing

11

entirely from memory. It was baffling to her.

She had only discovered her friend's secret talent while bringing a hand-knit baby blanket for Isabel at the end of her pregnancy. He'd sold Kallie an enormous drawing of a manatee for the price of materials – which was lucky since she couldn't have afforded his work now. Since then, Izzy had convinced her husband to start showing his work professionally, and he had been personally selected to paint one of the highly-popular murals in town. All while working regularly at The Lazy Gecko with Kallie, of course.

"Penny Jameson saw some of my work on display in Sarasota and asked me if I'd be willing to volunteer at the Clemons Center when it opens," Carlos told Kallie.

"Oh my gosh, that's so cool!" Kallie gushed. "You'd be so great with those kids. Can you make that drive, though?"

The Alexandra Clemons Center was being built in central Pasco County, which was an hour drive from Owhiro. It would offer arts studies to under-served kids in the community – starting with visual and musical arts.

"Well, it's still at least a year from opening. Maybe more. But I think I could get up there once a week." He nodded toward his wife. "Izzy thinks it's a good idea too."

"If anyone can teach those kids that you don't

need a degree from Julliard, or the Rhode Island School of Design, to be a great artist, it's Carlos," Isabel confirmed with a smile.

"You just need to make a killer Long Island Iced Tea," he added.

"I'm not sure that's *directly* related, but it's definitely a bonus."

Isabel and Kallie fell silent, snuggling the baby and watching Carlos create his beautiful artwork, until night fell over the little cottage completely. Kallie and Carlos made plans to meet at work one day that week, so she could answer any questions before she left town. Not much about bartending had changed in the decade that he'd been the night manager, but the ordering computers were new, and she thought he might want to catch up on the newest popular drinks.

"Have a great trip," Isabel called as Kallie waved goodbye and blew kisses to the baby.

"Don't worry about work," Carlos added. "I've got you covered."

Kallie drove home feeling relieved and finally ready for her amazing vacation.

* * * * *

With a couple of minutes to herself before they had to leave for the Port, Kallie had a chance to reflect on the past few months.

She'd always been proud of her resilience and self-sufficiency, and she'd been fine after the recent murder that had literally fallen in her lap. Perfectly fine, until she wasn't. After the initial shock and hoopla wore off, she'd started having the nightmares again.

Once she got up the nerve to admit this to Tess, her best friend had urged her to see a shrink. A professional therapist, to put it nicely. Being shaken up after something like that doesn't make you weak or crazy, Tess had insisted.

But Kallie really couldn't afford it, and she didn't know what she'd say to a therapist anyway.

I'm basically a therapist in my own job, as everyone constantly tells me. So maybe I could talk to another bartender instead, she reasoned.

Mike was game to listen, and he'd been right in the thick of the murder too. They'd been friends for years, and he'd always been a sympathetic ear and shoulder for her, with no ulterior motive. She didn't tell him about the occasional panic attacks, but he thought the nightmares and jumpiness were completely normal, considering the circumstances. More than normal, really.

Their talks helped a little, but mostly Kallie just kept busy. Between her job at The Lazy Gecko, volunteering at the local homeless shelter, learning new swing dances, and taking long walks with Sherman –

who had time to worry?

Working long hours is a reasonable replacement for deep soul-searching, right?

She hoped this cruise would finally give her a chance to completely relax.

"Are you ready to go?" Kallie's dad asked, tapping on her door and shaking her out of her reverie. "You said you were *almost* ready half an hour ago."

Kallie dragged her suitcases to the door. "I'm ready. I'm so excited, but I wish Sherman could come."

Her beloved dog sat patiently on the couch, looking a little dejected.

"I know, kiddo. But Anna and I will spoil him rotten and take him for lots of walks to see his friends. He'll be okay."

"And you won't give him too much bacon?"

"I make no promises regarding bacon..." her dad muttered, picking up her bags. "Besides, it's only a week. We'll be fine. And I've heard you can video chat from the ports, so you'll get to see each other."

Kallie laughed awkwardly, embarrassed at how relieved that thought made her feel.

"And don't forget your SPF 50 sunblock. You got that pasty skin from me, and I got the worst sunburn of my life in the Cayman Islands when you were a kid."

"I remember, Dad. I've got two bottles in my carry-on."

"Even burnt my eyelids," he added, with a shudder. "Did you see that detective friend of yours, to let him know you're going out of town?"

"We had breakfast on Tuesday, Dad." She knew her dad liked Detective Morrison, whom he'd met during the recent murder investigation. "I gave him your regards. Even though I know you two text each other like schoolkids."

"Well, it takes a small army to keep you girls out of trouble," her father quipped with a smile.

Neither of them made a secret of their friendship, and Kallie knew they texted about fishing and barbeque grills and Buccaneers football – and probably other, more serious topics, since they were both veterans. She suspected they talked about her sometimes, too. But she didn't feel the need to be nosy about it.

"Got everything?" her dad asked, walking away with her bags.

"I think so. Wow, Tess is going to be here in fifteen minutes, Dad! I can't believe it's time to go!"

Chapter Two

Tess and Kallie waited in the line to board the cruise ship for about half an hour, sipping bottled water and turning back to wave at Kallie's dad occasionally. It was still pretty hot outside – even though it was early November – but nowhere near as bad as the spring heat, and they were both wearing cute sundresses to make the most of the breeze. Kallie felt bad for the northerners who'd just flown in that day, still lugging their winter coats.

"I can't wait to jump in the pool," Tess grumbled.

"Oh, me too. I hope there's a slide into the deep end."

"There'll be a line of ten-year-olds a mile long. I'm just going to cannonball in from the side."

"That sounds amazing," Kallie sighed forlornly, fanning herself with a magazine from her carry-on bag. Ditto on the cannonball option."

"I can't believe we're fantasizing about how to jump into a swimming pool. You can tell it's been too long since either of us had a vacation." Tess laughed.

"Or even a decent swimming pool."

"Your dad got my mind stuck on drinking a piña colada," Tess added with a grin. "I'm getting one as soon as we're out of the pool."

"I can't wait to see the buffet. Especially the breakfast buffet!"

"Why is this line taking so long? We're going to drive ourselves crazy in five more minutes."

Kallie pinned up her auburn hair with a ballpoint pen as she melted in the heat. Working the night shift for so long had made her unaccustomed to the midday sun. She peered over the crowd and saw hundreds of other people grouchily suffering in front of them.

"Oh look, there's the ramp," Tess pointed out with relief.

"Man, this ship is enormous. It seemed like we were getting close to the ramp about three blocks ago!"

"This ship's tiny, compared to the ones that dock in Miami. It still looks like a whole floating city, though."

Kallie knew ships could only dock in Tampa if they fit under the Skyway Bridge – which limited their options. If they'd bought their own tickets, they probably would've taken a ship out of Port Canaveral instead, but their grand prize vacation was leaving from the smaller port in downtown Tampa. It still dwarfed all of the huge office buildings and looked almost like a hallucination against the city skyline.

"I hear they have a whole roller coaster in there. And a movie theater, I think?"

"I think the movie theater is outside, so you can watch it from the pool," Tess added.

"Oh, that's so cool! Tess, I would *never* have thought to take a cruise. It's such a touristy thing to do, you know? But this is going to be so much fun!"

"I know, me neither," her best friend replied with a grin. "When people told me they were going on a cruise, I always rolled my eyes like it was the dumbest thing. Now that we're here, I'm so excited. We're going to have a blast."

"And relax," Kallie added, happily.

"Yes! Relax," Tess replied with a sagely nod. "Definitely relax."

* * * * *

Finally they reached the check-in point and handed over all of their documentation and paperwork. Whatever was taking everyone else so long, Kallie and Tess apparently didn't have the same problem, because they were approved and heading up the ramp in less than two minutes. They both squealed in excitement as they ran uphill, toward the main deck, dragging their bags behind them.

"We're officially on *vaca-a-a-a-ation*," Kallie sang out loud.

They reached the deck and were quickly pointed in the direction of the lobby by a crew member.

Almost all of the nearby passengers seemed just as dazzled as Kallie and Tess. The brilliant blue Florida sky and sparkling waters emphasized the glamour of the ship. It might not have been the newest or biggest ship in the world, but it was beautiful.

The doors to the lobby slid open, and it looked like they were walking into a New York City hotel. Kallie wasn't sure what she'd expected – probably something more like her mother's golfing clubhouse – but it certainly wasn't this old-fashioned luxury.

"Wow, that chandelier is bigger than my car," Kallie whispered.

"It's bigger than our first apartment after college," Tess replied.

"My car's bigger than that apartment, too. It didn't even have room for a dinner table."

The polished marble check-in desks were fully staffed, and they only waited a minute before being called forward.

"Hi, we're Kalliope Brooks and Tess Russo."

The receptionist pulled up their reservation and noted cheerfully that they were the WBUZ contest winners. "The cruise line has a great relationship with

George and Celeste," she added. "They've even come out for a trip with us before. It's a great prize."

She didn't elaborate but handed over a pair of room keys and a brochure with a map of the whole ship, and then gave them directions up to their room.

"If you get lost, just ask anyone in a cruise ship uniform."

"Lost?" Kallie whispered to Tess.

"I'm sure it happens all the time. Let's see if we can find the elevators."

Luckily, they found their way without getting lost or even confused – though they saw two families talking with employees who were either pointing or guiding them in the right direction.

"I hope our room's nice," Tess whispered, as they crowded into the elevator with a bewildered-looking family of six.

"It was free, and we're not going to spend any time in there, so even if it's a broom closet, I'll be excited," Kallie whispered back.

"I still hope it's nice."

"Me too!" Kallie laughed.

Stepping off the elevator onto their floor, they walked quickly back toward the center of the ship and looked down into the decks below, shocked at how far it was.

"Wow, this place is huge."

In her usual curious form, Tess had already unfolded the brochure and read all of the details. "They have six pools, and two indoor tennis courts," she pointed out, then turned to walk back toward their room. "Not to mention all of the shows and restaurants and attractions. It looks like they have a climbing rock wall, too."

"I'll skip the climbing rock wall," Kallie cringed.

"I might want to try it," Tess answered, squinting at the tiny photo.

"I'll cheer you on, as long as I can bring a plate of waffles."

"They probably serve waffles in the gym," Tess reassured her with a laugh. "I've heard it's all-food-all-the-time. I'll bet the prize for making it to the top of the rock wall is a grande chimichanga."

Kallie grinned. "In that case, maybe I'll try it after all."

"528, this is our room," Tess said, quietly, stopping in front of the door.

"That wasn't so hard to find," Kallie answered, rolling her bags up to the door. "We didn't even need a sherpa."

"I hope it's nice–" Tess stood still for another nervous moment with the key card in her hand, clearly expecting the worst.

Kallie snatched it away and quickly unlocked

the door, and they both stood in awe.

"How can they give away a room like this for *free*?" Tess asked breathlessly.

Their room was a suite with two queen beds and a separate, cozy sitting room with two couches and a large table. There was even a small kitchen with a bar counter and velvet-covered stools. Both rooms had balconies, and Kallie immediately ran over and pulled open the drapes to see the view.

Since they were still in port, there wasn't much to see except the endless concrete of the parking lot. Kallie knew it would be beautiful by afternoon, though. Opening the sliding glass door, she stepped out onto the balcony – peering down at the hot and grumpy travelers below, still standing in the long line – and danced in place like a joyful schoolgirl.

Kallie and Tess unpacked and hung up their eveningwear carefully and then lounged around their spacious suite like seagoing princesses for a little while. Finally, they felt the ship start to move – then they hurried back upstairs to see the final exciting view, as the ship officially left Tampa Bay.

A few tendrils of fog slipped around the ship as it passed under the enormous Skyway Bridge, and the passengers on deck cheered loudly. Kallie wondered what the drivers climbing the towering, seemingly treacherous bridge must think, to see the ship so close.

I'd have a heart attack, if it was me. It probably makes for an interesting view though.

Luckily there was no heavy fog, which would have delayed their departure from the port. It was much too dangerous to sail a ship under the famous bridge in the fog, and ships were sometimes delayed for hours on very foggy days.

They turned and watched the bridge slowly disappear behind them, and the crowd gradually dispersed from the upper deck.

"Ready to go back downstairs?" Tess asked.

"I'm hungry. I didn't have time to eat anything before we left this morning."

"Gee, I'm not sure if they have any food, Kallie," Tess replied with mock seriousness. "Only about six varieties of every food that was ever invented."

"Great, I could go for pancakes."

"Pancakes it is, then."

"And an egg roll."

"I'm sure we can find both. I could eat an egg roll myself, now that you mention it."

"Do you think Sherman misses me yet?"

"I think your dad is probably raising Sherm's cholesterol by ten points, stuffing him full of bacon. But yes. While he's not eating, I'm sure he misses you."

Kallie's shoulders slumped a little.

"Don't you start. Sherman's going to be fine. Your dad and Anna will spoil him rotten, so he doesn't have time to worry – and he'll be even more excited to see you when you get home. Now let's get you some food and a cheesy tabloid magazine and a lounge chair by the pool."

They walked toward the elevators as the last of Tampa Bay disappeared into the distance behind them.

* * * * *

After a quick snack and an even quicker dip in the pool, Kallie and Tess finally found themselves sitting in decadent lounge chairs on the ship's main deck, exactly like they'd both dreamed. They were distracted when another pair of women sat down next to them.

"I love your shoes," one of them said to Kallie, who was engrossed in a fabulously trashy tabloid magazine.

Looking down at her old but colorfully striped Converse tennis shoes, Kallie was surprised at the compliment, until she glanced over at the speaker. The other woman, a slim, freckled southerner with strawberry blonde hair and an infectious smile, was wearing a pair of matching low-top Converse shoes with red and orange flames up the side.

"Thanks, I love yours too!" She grinned back at

her style twin.

"I'm Missy, and this is my sister Laura," she gestured at her companion, a pretty brunette with blue eyes that perfectly matched her sister's, who waved happily. "We're from Atlanta."

"Gee, I'd never guess you two were related," Kallie laughed. The two of them were both pretty but looked completely different except for their identical sky-blue eyes.

"Everyone says that. It's the eyes, right?"

"It's uncanny," Kallie answered, but she changed the subject quickly, knowing they'd heard it a million times before. "My mother always made fun of me for wearing Converse. She said they made my giant feet look like canoes."

"She sounds charming," Missy replied with a sarcastic laugh.

"You have no idea," Tess mumbled in agreement from her lounge chair. Kallie's mother was difficult at the best of times and cuttingly critical at the worst.

"It didn't help that I'd wear them until they literally fell apart," Kallie added with a laugh, "and my toes were sticking out of holes in the sides. But she thought all young ladies should wear high heels."

"No thanks," Missy grimaced. "I did my time in hose and heels, working in an office in Manhattan for seven years. Navy pencil skirts, the whole traumatic rigamarole. Never again."

"I don't mind them for special occasions, but I'm on my feet all day, tending bar, and it's uncomfortable enough in flats. Besides, I'd break my neck trying to hurry."

Tess and Kallie chatted with Missy and Laura for a while about the ship and the relief of being on vacation. They went back to reading and napping in the sun, but agreed to meet for dinner that evening, in the Seven Seas dining room, before their new friends left the pool.

* * * * *

At their First Night dinner, which turned out to be pretty formal and boring, they found that Tess and Laura had a few friends in common in Georgia – where Tess's parents lived. Apart from a love of Chuck Taylor shoes, Missy and Kallie also loved the same music and both adored dogs. After chatting and laughing a little too loudly for the dining room and deciding it was too early to retire, they made their way to a nightclub playing dance music.

Not long after arriving and dancing to a few songs, though, they found the place had become nearly empty.

"Where is everybody?" Missy asked. "I thought this was supposed to be the most popular dance club on the ship?"

Kallie walked up to the bar and shouted over the pointlessly loud music, "Where did everyone go? It's like a ghost town in here."

The bartender shrugged and rolled his eyes. "No idea. It was crowded ten minutes ago. There must be something going on out in the hallway." He nodded toward the main door. "They sometimes have giveaways. Or who knows? Maybe there's someone famous on board?"

Kallie started walking toward the door, but Tess grabbed her hand. "I have a bad feeling about this, Kal."

"Is it because I said 'ghost town?'" She made a spooky face and held up her arms menacingly.

"You're such a weirdo. Fine, let's go." But she didn't drop Kallie's hand.

As they reached the main entrance, they could see that the crowd had, indeed, gathered in the hallway. People were still curiously walking out of other doorways from nearby restaurants and bars. But there was nothing going on – no announcer or cheerful entertainer offering prizes. No pop star or reality show actress signing autographs.

"Nothing fun," Missy agreed. "Should we go back?"

Kallie nodded and was turning to join her, when she heard Laura hiss, "Oh no, it's my date."

Being a bit taller than most women, Kallie instinctively stepped in front of her new friend. She wasn't even sure what the guy looked like. Scanning around, she didn't see any strange men staring back at them. A large group of revelers, including several young men, stood nearby – all covered in silver and gold metallic confetti – but they didn't look toward Kallie and her friends.

Laura quickly slipped off her high-heeled sandals to make herself less visible and peeked around Kallie's shoulder. "Sorry, that was so awkward," she laughed. "I'm having dinner with that guy tomorrow night, and I'm not wearing makeup or anything. Thank you for hiding me."

"No problem," Kallie replied. "I've hidden from a few guys in my life."

Unfortunately, I was hiding from the last one because he was threatening to kill me for trespassing, not because I forgot to wear mascara, she thought to herself.

"Where's everyone going?" Tess asked as they watched the crowd shift toward one end of the hallway.

"I don't know, but my date's going with them. So I'm not going down there unless they're giving away free chocolate-covered Cadillacs."

Missy laughed and shook her head at her sister's silliness, but she also stood on her toes to see what was so intriguing.

Most of the people seemed to be crowded around the all-you-can-eat buffet next to the railing.

Kallie wondered if she could've somehow misjudged the time they'd spent in the dance club – perhaps they were already lining up for breakfast? But she looked at her watch and saw that it was just after one a.m.

"What's going on?" Tess charmingly asked another group of young women, who were standing nearby.

"Something in that corner. We couldn't get close enough to see," a blonde woman in pink sequins answered. "I don't think the restaurant is even open at this hour."

"Let's go back to the club," the blonde's friend complained. "I can't see anything from here, and I want to dance. They're playing '90s music, and I need another chocolate martini."

"In a minute," the first girl replied, eyes still glued on the opposite corner, as if she would suddenly be able to see what was going on. An old Britney Spears song started playing, and the complaining girl hurried past them, back to the dance floor.

They tried to peek over the crowd, but more people were gathering, and they couldn't get a look. No one seemed sure what was happening, but they didn't want to leave, either – and there was a lot of nervous talking but no explanation. Kallie could see the flash of a few camera phones.

They were about to give up when the onboard security team arrived – looking very serious and speaking into their walkie-talkies – and started breaking up the crowd and sending people back to their rooms.

"We can't have this many people in a confined area, folks. It's a fire hazard. Go back to your activities – there's nothing to see here."

Once the crowd thinned a little, Kallie could finally see what everyone had been staring at. In the restaurant, on the huge buffet table – which just a few hours ago had held dozens of bagels, pounds of chopped fruit, and hundreds of cocktail shrimp – a man was stretched across the faux marble, awkwardly splayed out.

His face was turned away from them, but his hands were visible, hanging over the edges of the table. One shoe lay on the floor below his sock-clad foot.

After a few minutes, the remaining gawkers wandered off, ready to dance or head for bed, giggling about the drunk guy and the free booze on the ship. But Kallie had seen this before. She already knew he was dead.

Chapter Three

Long accustomed to waking up at the crack of dawn to take Sherman out for a walk, sleeping late wasn't a common experience for Kallie. She sprang awake automatically the next morning.

Tess wasn't usually a late sleeper either, but Kallie wasn't going to wake her up. She considered sneaking onto the balcony but didn't want to disturb her. It had been ages since either of them had found the time and money for a vacation. Her best friend slept quietly in the cozy nearby bed in their huge, glorious suite.

I wish someone had told me when I was seven that I'd have a real best friend. She'd felt different and weird as a kid. It seemed as if everyone else had better, cooler friends, until Tess came along in fifth grade. The other kids might've had better lunch boxes and backpacks, but who else had a bestie that would stick with them through thick and thin? Even, one day, through a murder?

Or maybe two? She added to herself.

Don't you dare think about that right now, Kalliope Brooks. You were stressed out by the crowd and overreacted for no reason. This is your first morning of your first real vacation in years, so don't ruin it!

As if on cue, Tess opened one eye and smiled. "I think I'm slept out."

Kallie turned on her bedside lamp and stretched, and then plodded to the in-room coffee maker with a yawn. "Me too." She spun the rack of coffee pods and grabbed one at random. "I got Marvelous Minty Mocha," she announced. "Pick your poison."

"I'll just take a Superbly Boring Light Roast, if you have one," Tess answered over the coffee machine's burbling noises, reaching for her phone. "And I recorded a video of Sherm for you before we left."

Kallie jumped over her bed and snatched the phone away. "I miss him so much!"

"I'm sure he misses you too. But you know your dad's feeding him four slices of pepperoni pizza for every meal. And probably cheesecake for dessert."

"Yeah, he'll probably have completely forgotten me when I get back," Kallie replied, watching the new video of her dog tilting his head at the camera, then popping his mismatched floppy ears up and waving his paw. "Aww, high five, little buddy. I'll be back soon."

"The brochure says we can video conference once we get into each port, so you won't need to survive the whole trip on one video," Tess laughed. She sipped her coffee as Kallie looked for something to wear. "In the meantime, let's get some breakfast and then stake out a poolside spot in the shade. You don't need any more sun!"

* * * * *

When Kallie and Tess made their way back to the upper deck that morning, the mysterious restaurant was still closed. The buffet table had obviously been cleaned – it was practically gleaming in the reflected light from the hallway. The smell of bleach and pine cleaner hung heavily in the air.

A janitor was just pushing away a mop and bucket, and the swinging door to the kitchen closed behind him. He must've scrubbed the floor, but Kallie knew she hadn't seen any blood last night. So maybe it was just a normal morning cleaning. *And maybe I imagined the whole thing*, Kallie thought to herself again.

If so, she wasn't the only one. A few small clusters of people gathered in the hallway outside the restaurant, whispering among themselves. A woman giggled nervously nearby, high-pitched and jarring.

"Did you see the same thing I saw, Tess?" Kallie asked quietly.

"I'm not sure," Tess replied, sounding concerned. "I'm not really sure what we saw."

"Why else would all these people be standing around, whispering?"

"Well, there's one easy way to find out the answer to *that* question—" Tess replied with a wink, and then suddenly plastered on a bright smile and turned away. "Excuse me," she called cheerfully to a group of whispering women. "Do you know when this buffet's opening? We really liked their Denver omelets!"

The circle of women closed around Tess like a gang of hyenas, and one blonde whispered, "There was a guy in there last night, on the table. We thought he was just really drunk, but Jannie thinks he was... DEAD!" She hissed the last word in the loudest whisper ever. Tess reached behind and snatched Kallie's sleeve, dragging her into the gossip circle.

"Really?" Tess whispered back.

"Jannie had a roommate in college who was a nursing student, so she would totally know a dead body when she saw it," the lady continued. She gestured toward a tall brunette, who was apparently Jannie. The brunette nodded excitedly.

"Oh, *totally*!" Tess agreed, then glanced at Kallie and raised a sarcastic eyebrow. "Was there a lot of blood and stuff?"

"No, he just looked drunk," the blonde answered with a frown and a shrug.

"Were there any cops?"

"I don't think cruises have cops. There were just

some security guys. But we saw them push back the crowd to let a doctor in, so it must have been serious."

Kallie and Tess hadn't seen a doctor, but the blonde was right – if the man had simply been drunk, the ship's doctor wouldn't have been called.

"What happened after *that?*" Tess pretended to be breathlessly engrossed by the blonde's lame, exaggerated story, but Kallie was still really curious about what had happened and hoped there might be a hint amidst the hyperbole. She thought Tess was wondering the same thing, despite her annoyance with the gossip.

"After the doctor went in, they pulled down a big metal door, so we couldn't see anything else." Kallie hadn't noticed a garage-style roll-down door, but it made sense that they would be installed. "Then the staff made us all leave, so we went back to our rooms. Do you think they have a *morgue* on board?"

Kallie saw Tess flinch at the sudden morbid direction the conversation had turned, and followed her as she broke away from the little group. "I really don't know, but we don't want to eat in a buffet where someone was sick or dead. We'll try another floor. Have a great day," Tess called back to them as she and Kallie hurried away.

* * * * *

Still whispering about the previous night's creepy but indeterminate scene, Kallie and Tess made their way down to find a spot by the pool. They had both forgotten about breakfast for the moment, but Tess wanted more coffee. Stopping at a kiosk, she ordered an iced mocha and looked to Kallie for her order. Checking the menu, Kallie ordered a strawberry-mango smoothie instead.

As the blender buzzed to life, they leaned on the nearby railing to wait.

"The cruise staff is perfectly capable of caring for one drunk guy. It's practically their main job description. There must have been something really wrong if they called the doctor," Kallie considered out loud.

Please convince me that I imagined the whole thing, Bestie, so we can go back to sun and fun.

"Sure, but it could've been anything. He might've injured himself when he fell over the table. Even knocked himself out. Or it could've been a heart attack or a seizure or something. And they would've rolled down the door for his privacy while the doctor checked him out."

"That sounds reasonable, I guess."

"We didn't hear a helicopter, though," Tess continued after some more thought. "I think they evacuate people who get really sick."

Kallie sighed sadly at that logic. "I just know he

was dead, Tess."

"I'm not sure you're the best person to make that diagnosis," Tess answered with a nudge, but also a gentle smile. "I think they'd have to announce it if he died, anyway. We aren't the only people who saw him, and they wouldn't want to start a panic."

The barista topped Kallie's smoothie with whipped cream and a strawberry and handed the decadent drink over.

After one sip, Kallie was jubilant. "This is amazing!" she beamed at the barista. "Seriously, I think this is the best smoothie I've ever had. What did you add?"

"Nothing special, we just get really fresh fruit and yogurt," the young woman smiled with pride. "And the honey is local to one of the villages where we stop on the cruise. You can pick up a jar at the dock."

Kallie passed the drink to Tess, who took a sip and agreed. "I can't believe there's not a huge line at your kiosk."

The girl smiled shyly but shook her head. "I just took this job because my husband is a deckhand. He loves it out here on the sea, but I don't like the crowds–" She stopped herself suddenly, blushing furiously. "What am I saying? You don't want to hear my problems. Please don't–"

"Don't worry, we won't tell anyone— about your secretly insane smoothies," Kallie reassured her with a laugh. "But we'll be back for more."

The kiosk line was growing behind them, so they moved away, sipping their drinks while they each silently considered the situation.

"When do you think they'll announce it, if the guy really was dead?" Kallie finally asked as they continued on toward the pool.

"Are we talking about this again?" Tess sighed. "There's no loudspeaker, so they'd probably print out a letter and slip it under everyone's door tonight. With an email address for grief counseling at the end, I'm sure. But we don't know he's dead, Kal."

"He looked—"

Tess grabbed her hand – *just as she'd grabbed it the night before, saying she had a bad feeling about the empty club*, Kallie remembered – and reassured her, "He's probably just fine. Probably sleeping off a whopper of a hangover and dreaming of pancakes with tequila syrup."

The dazzling blue sky seemed to erupt above them, as they walked from the darkened hallway onto the deck. As the breeze tossed their hair, Tess let out an audible, happy sigh.

"Have I mentioned hooray for vacation?" she asked, twirling on the toes of one flip-flop.

"Yes, but I think we can both safely repeat it. Hooray for vacation!" Kallie agreed.

A gorgeous spot in the shade called to them, and they collapsed onto a pair of lounge chairs, slathered on the sunscreen, and left all thoughts of the previous night behind.

* * * * *

"Oh my gosh, Tess. I'm so sunburned!" Kallie stared at the mirror and pulled the strap of her bathing suit off her shoulder. The white skin underneath showed a vivid contrast against the bright red sun damage.

"You and your pasty white skin wanted to sit by the pool," Tess mumbled as she squatted down to dig through her suitcase.

"I used SPF 50," Kallie replied, poking at her arm, and then leaning toward the mirror to squint at the bridge of her nose. "That's usually enough. And we were in the *shade*!"

"The sun reflecting off the water probably made it worse. Does it hurt?"

"Not too much, actually."

"Good, it's probably not as bad as it looks. Go take a cold shower to stop the burning." Tess held up a travel-size bottle full of neon green goo. "Luckily, someone remembered to bring the aloe, Vampirella."

"You're a lifesaver!"

Tess stuck the bottle of aloe in the mini fridge to cool it down even more and shooed her best friend away. "Quick, we're going to be late for dinner. The radio station set up some kind of promotion tonight, and we need to be there on time."

"Promotion? We don't have to make a speech or anything, do we?" Kallie called back from the shower a few minutes later.

"No, I think they're doing another giveaway, but they'll probably want pictures of us. What are you going to wear?"

"Oh, if they're taking pictures, then probably that dark blue dress." Kallie could hear the wooden hangers clunking together as Tess looked through the closet.

"Got it," Tess yelled back. "How's the sunburn?"

"Much better under the cold water. Can I stay in here all night?"

"Not a chance. I'm not going to this thing alone. Besides, you're better at these publicity things than I am, with your wily bartender-slash-therapist skills."

Kallie laughed. "I'll hypnotize them into giving us free tickets to Busch Gardens, too."

"Perfect! Besides, I'm hungry. Hurry up!"

Kallie had just finished dousing her skin in cold aloe vera gel and changing clothes, ten minutes later, when a knock at the suite door surprised them.

Kallie looked at Tess, who shrugged. They weren't expecting anyone, but Kallie cautiously walked over to check the door. Looking through the peephole, she saw a tall, serious-looking older man in the hallway, dressed in the cruise ship's security uniform. She cracked the door open, without unlatching the swing bar, to see what he needed.

"Yes?"

"I'm with the ship's security team," he answered, holding up an ID badge. "There's been an incident on board, and we're speaking personally with the passengers who may have witnessed it."

Kallie reached out through the crack in the door and swiped the badge out of his hand, to his obvious surprise, and turned back to Tess. They both looked at it for a minute, conferring silently, and Tess nodded that it looked legitimate. Kallie unlatched and opened the door to let him in.

"Is it about the guy in the restaurant?" Kallie asked quietly, feeling that recently familiar sense of dread rise up in her stomach.

"Yes," the guard replied, taking his ID back from her with a frown. He had a greying mustache and sharp grey eyes, and he looked a little like she pictured cops in New York looked in 1890. "We're not making a ship-wide announcement, but several people saw him, so we wanted to address it before the gossip spreads too far."

"Is he dead?" Tess asked, bluntly.

"I'm afraid so. It's against the cruise line's policy to announce deaths, and there are usually healthcare privacy implications, as well. But federal agents will be boarding the ship when we reach Cozumel, and they'll need to speak with everyone who was identified nearby."

"Federal agents? Don't you just fly the body back to the US?" Tess asked.

"When someone dies by natural causes, yes. But it appears there may have been foul play involved," the man replied. Kallie was surprised at how calmly he said those strange words.

This must not be as rare as it would seem.

Kallie looked at Tess with an expression that shouted: *I told you so!*

"Foul play?" Tess replied, frowning. "Wait, you mean *murder*? On this ship?"

"I'm afraid so," he repeated, calmly.

Kallie felt her heart flutter in her throat and swayed dizzily for a second. She touched the wall until the room stopped spinning.

"We thought it was a heart attack or something," Tess gasped, taking a step back. "Hang on, surely you don't think we're *suspects*?

"It's more likely that you could be witnesses, actually. This ship seems very large, but there are a lot of eyes in a closed space. It's almost impossible to commit a crime unseen, and even harder to escape." His voice was friendly, but his grey eyes were flinty and unyielding. Kallie was pretty sure they were still potential suspects, as far as he was concerned.

"What did you mean by people who were 'identified nearby?' How did you know we were there? He wasn't near this wing of the ship, and there were dozens of people."

"Fifty-four people, actually, who were in close enough proximity to have possibly seen something useful," he corrected her.

Kallie and Tess looked at each other, and then back at him.

"Our IT Department was able to identify everyone in that section of the hallway," he explained, "and we're—"

"You have an *IT Department*?" Kallie interrupted.

"Of course. They mostly handle the billing computers and the entertainment scheduling, but they were able to repurpose the facial recognition software from the casino." He sounded proud of their resourcefulness, and Kallie suddenly realized that this non-descript guy was in charge – probably the head of security. "Everyone has an IT Department, you know," he added. "We just have a particularly good one."

A young woman in a matching security uniform approached him in the doorway, gesturing that she was moving on to the next identified passenger's room. He nodded in acknowledgement, and then turned back to continue his questioning.

"Did you see or hear anything leading up to the gathering in the hallway?" he asked Kallie and Tess.

"No, we had a late dinner and we'd just arrived at the nightclub when we saw the crowd. Most of them seemed to think he was just drunk," Kallie replied.

The guard nodded but didn't ask what *she'd* thought. He seemed satisfied with the reply.

"The fifty-four of you will need to stay in your cabins when we reach the port at Cozumel, and prepare for a formal interview, but we'll release you as quickly as possible. If you're signed up for an excursion, we'll ask them to wait for you." He pulled two business cards out of his pocket and handed them over. "Give me a call if you think of anything or have any questions. Calls go directly to my cell phone," he added, touching an outer pocket of his jacket, "so I'm always available."

"We'll do that," Tess answered, glancing at the card, "Officer Reilly."

"Officer Navarro will be glad to help you, as well. She was a lieutenant with the San Diego police, so she actually outranks me."

"Not out here on the high seas, I don't, Reilly," the other officer answered with a smile, from a few doors away. The pretty hazel-eyed brunette looked about twenty-five, but must have been in her mid-forties to have that background, Kallie realized. Navarro offered her card as well, but added, "You won't need my help, with Officer Reilly looking out for you. But I'm here if anything comes up." She moved off down the hallway again.

"Are you all police officers?" Kallie asked.

"HappySail doesn't hire anyone for security unless they have a police background. Preferably both civilian and military."

"That's reassuring," Tess replied with a nod.

"We'll contact you if we think of anything," Kallie added.

He thanked them and walked away after his fellow security officer, as Tess closed the cabin door and carefully set both locks and twisted the bolt.

"Well, here we go again," Kallie moaned, hugging her arms across her chest.

"Hey, lighten up. At least we're not in danger this time." Tess laughed quietly, pulling out a flippy teal dress for dinner.

Kallie pouted as she grudgingly started applying mascara in the mirror, suddenly dreading the radio station event.

"We have another whole day before we get to Cozumel, and nothing but free time," Tess added with a playful but gentle smile, obviously trying to calm and distract her worried best friend as much as possible.

"Think we can solve the murder before the feds get here?"

Chapter Four

The radio station dinner was entertaining and relatively quick. Tess was thrilled to find that she didn't need to make a speech – the announcer shone a spotlight on the two of them at their table and they waved happily. A few cameras flashed, and that was all.

Then it was just an hour of free margaritas and dancing, a few more fun publicity photos, and happily meeting other passengers. Kallie felt her earlier worry sliding away, as they danced to Tess's obscure contest-winning song, *'Your Tentative Love.'*

There was a quick raffle, and someone really did win tickets to Busch Gardens – but it wasn't Kallie. Tess won a hundred-dollar gift card for onboard shopping, but neither of them could think of anything to spend it on, since everything was already pre-paid by the radio station.

Two more photos with the station's representative, and they were done. A young lady handed them a pair of WBUZ t-shirts as they left the dining room.

"These are cute!" Kallie laughed, holding the shirt up to herself over her dress. The design on the soft navy blue shirts showed a cartoonish cruise ship shaped like the radio station's call letters, along with sea birds and dolphins.

They walked over to rendezvous with Missy and Laura, near the restaurants – but since their new friends had also already eaten, they decided to go back to the suite instead. After a stop for snacks and drinks at a buffet on the way, they settled in, and changed from dresses and heels into shorts and t-shirts. They turned on a movie and played Pictionary for a while – which Kallie's dad insisted they bring along – but later switched to cards.

Kallie shuffled the deck and then dealt them out. Tess immediately picked hers up, but Missy and Laura were still talking.

"I'm glad you ditched that guy to stay with us," Missy said between bites of popcorn. "This is way better."

"I can see him in the morning; he was getting way too obsessive," Laura agreed. "Ooh, this is the best part of the movie, would you turn it up a little?"

Kallie turned up the sound on the huge TV, as a vintage Vespa zoomed across the screen. "Pick up your cards, ladies. My dad would be smacking you with a flyswatter by now."

"It's true," Tess agreed with a nod. "He's very serious about his Rummy."

They both apologized and grabbed their cards.

"What do you ladies think about meeting a guy on a cruise?" Laura asked.

"Ugh, bad idea," Tess answered immediately.

"Best case, it turns out great and he's your absolute soulmate, but he lives in Alaska and you never see him again," Kallie added. "Worst case, he's annoying and smelly, and you can't get away from him for three days."

"See, that's what I'm saying," Missy answered with a laugh.

Audrey Hepburn and Gregory Peck kept talking in the background as the girls played their hands. They were betting with spare change, since Kallie had forgotten to bring poker chips.

"I'm betting my last twenty-five cents, and I'm out of cards," Missy announced triumphantly, throwing down her last card on the stack and displaying the rest.

Tess quietly countered, "You forgot to call Rummy, darlin'."

"Oh no! You and your dishy shipboard romance," she jokingly snapped at her sister. "You cost me my last quarter. I'm destitute!"

Laura apologized and grabbed her purse, digging to the bottom. "I have a quarter, six pennies, and a linty book of stamps in here. They're all yours. No more talking about random guys, I swear."

"What did you mean, when you said that guy

was getting obsessive, earlier?" Tess inquired. "If you don't mind my asking."

"When I told him I wanted to spend the evening with my ladies, he got all pouty and said he had plans for us. But when I asked him what they were, he just said 'nothing' and walked away," Laura answered, rolling her eyes.

"Well he couldn't have spent a lot of money on it, whatever it was – practically everything's free on the ship," Missy added sensibly.

"Sounds like you dodged a whiny bullet, girlfriend," Kallie concluded as she placed her discard. "Your turn."

They played a few more hands, while eating snacks and chatting, until the game paused again. Missy had been staring vacantly at her cards for a minute or two, and Kallie tried to shake her out of it.

"Hey, are you okay?"

"What?!" her new friend started. "I'm fine! Sorry, I was just..."

"Still thinking about Laura's pouty date?" Kallie asked.

"Oh, no. I was just... Did anyone from the cruise staff talk to you today?"

Kallie and Tess looked at each other quickly. Kallie knew the sisters had been with them in the club but hadn't realized that they'd also been close to the restaurant. Close enough to be on Reilly's camera, apparently.

"Yeah," Kallie replied quietly. "Did they talk to you guys too?"

"A female security guard came to our room to ask us some questions. She wasn't very nice."

"She said a guy died," Laura interjected, "and she was acting like it was our fault."

"We were just dancing," Missy added, looking sad. "We didn't do anything wrong."

"I'm sure they don't think you did it. They have to be really blunt, so the real killer thinks he's busted and confesses."

"*Killer?*" Missy asked with a gasp, eyes widening.

"Oh." Kallie blushed even redder than her auburn hair. "Oh, you didn't ask them about it?"

"I keep trying to tell you that you aren't *like* normal people," Tess whispered to Kallie with a quiet laugh and a nudge.

"Everyone was saying the guy was drunk last night. The security guard was really suspicious, so we thought maybe he overdosed or something," Missy explained. "We don't do drugs or anything, and we would never—"

"The guy was murdered, Missy. We asked the security chief, and he told us a little bit about it."

"Great," Missy sighed, sliding toward her sister on the couch. "Murdered."

"But they're going to solve it, and we don't need to worry," Tess added, cheerfully. "And they definitely don't think it's *your* fault, I promise."

Kallie nodded and repeated, "We promise."

"They've probably solved it already, actually. So let's keep playing," Tess added with a smile. "I'm going to order something from room service – do you like fondue?"

"Yes!" the sisters both answered in unison, and then laughed.

With the mood lightened a little, Tess called in the room service order while the others got back to their card game.

* * * * *

Missy and Laura had just left, after cautiously checking the hallway for axe murderers, when the desk phone in their suite rang. Kallie looked at Tess quizzically.

"Our room service was delivered over an hour ago. Maybe they're finally calling everyone about the murder."

"Oh, or maybe they really did catch the killer already, and they're letting us off the ship on schedule in Cozumel," Kallie sighed with cautious relief, reaching for the phone.

"Hopefully," Tess answered, not sounding convinced.

"Hello?"

"Wha— Who are you? Put Mikey on the phone," a woman's shocked voice answered. Kallie heard her say "It's some chick" to someone in the background.

"I think you have the wrong number," Kallie replied, starting to hang up.

"Whatever, lady. Look, put Mikey on the phone. He's my husband—"

"I'm thrilled for you. He sounds like a prince, but there's no Mikey here."

"I'm gonna kick—"

Kallie hung up, looking at Tess again, this time shaking her head.

"What was that?"

"Some crazy woman looking for her husband. She just threatened me when I said he wasn't here."

"Looks like we're talking to security again," Tess replied with a grimace.

"Why doesn't *anyone* on this stupid boat understand that we're supposed to be having fun?" Kallie grumbled in annoyance.

"And why are we always on a first-name basis

with the cops, lately?"

"Just lucky, I guess," Kallie answered, already dialing Officer Edmund Reilly's direct number.

* * * * *

Reilly was at their door in fifteen minutes, but he apparently hoped they'd thought of some other detail about the murder.

"You got a *what*? From *who*?"

"It was just a wrong number, but it came from someone on the cruise, and she threatened me," Kallie explained. "Not that I think she was the murderer or anything, but—"

"But tempers seem to be getting a little frayed, yes," Reilly replied with a nod. "All of the phone records are computerized, so I can look up the room number from my office and have a little chat with your drunk and jealous friend."

"Thank you, I appreciate it."

"You didn't happen to remember seeing or hearing anything suspicious around the time of the murder, since we last spoke?" Reilly added, sounding hopeful.

"I'm afraid not," Kallie answered with a frown. "We didn't see any blood; I remember that. And one of the other bystanders mentioned that too, this morning.

That there was no blood."

"You talked to other passengers about it?" Reilly asked, with concern.

"We just saw a small crowd around the restaurant this morning and wondered if they'd heard anything," Tess clarified. "There was a lot of gossip, but not much else. Kallie knew he was—"

Don't say it. Please don't tell him, Tess. He'll think I'm crazy.

As if Tess had read her mind, she completely changed direction, "We thought he'd had some kind of medical episode, which I believe we mentioned earlier. But, I mean, what if he'd had some kind of reaction to the food? A peanut allergy to something that wasn't labeled? Or food poisoning? Salmonella or listeria or something?"

"So we were just checking, to make sure it was safe to keep eating the food," Kallie agreed, nodding.

The security officer stood silently for a moment, tapping his pen against the notepad, and apparently considering his options. Then he nodded, shut the door, and sat down on a barstool. "It's nothing like that. The HappySail CEO was afraid of *exactly* this kind of rumor, especially in this high-speed news era of blogging and social media."

He looked exhausted and frustrated, and they waited for him to continue.

"This is a family-friendly cruise line, and any

suggestion of contamination could tank the stock before we even get to Mexico. Not that I own any stock," he added with a weary smile. "But I have my orders." After another moment, he closed his notebook and added, quickly, "Look, we don't have a medical examiner on the ship, obviously, but the doctor thinks he was poisoned."

Tess and Kallie looked at each other, surprised, and Tess asked, "You can tell us that?"

"Morrison never told us *anything*," Kallie whispered to her, grumpily.

"I can't tell you anything about the victim. All that stuff is protected by federal medical privacy laws," he quickly clarified. He then added with an annoyed eye roll, "Although I'm sure you've heard his name by now, on the gossip grapevine. He's pretty famous in your neck of the Central Florida woods."

Reilly had checked their IDs earlier, but presumably he'd checked dozens of them in the past two days. Kallie hadn't heard the victim's name, but she was impressed that the officer even remembered where they lived.

"But in this case," he continued, "I've been cleared to discuss the possible cause of death, to the extent that we suppress any panic. The ship's board of directors was notified last night, and they're very concerned about creating an *incident*."

Kallie noticed that he scowled at that last word.

"Poison? Isn't that considered a 'woman's weapon?'" Tess asked.

"Usually," Reilly answered, sounding dismissive. Kallie could tell he was trying to politely end the discussion. "On dry land, almost always."

"Dry land? Oh, I see," Tess nodded, after a moment's thought. "But on a ship, it's the only weapon that might make it through security."

Reilly didn't answer, but stood up to leave.

"And your doctor thinks his food was poisoned?" Kallie asked. "Wouldn't that be awfully risky in an all-you-can-eat buffet? You could accidentally kill the wrong person. Or *a lot* of wrong people."

"Oh, no. It wasn't his dinner that was poisoned," Reilly sighed with barely concealed annoyance at her tenacity. "See, this is exactly why the cruise line wants us to intervene – against our standard rules. It wasn't the food that was poisoned. There's no general risk to the public."

"How do you poison someone at a buffet like that, without putting it in the food?" Tess asked, sarcastically, starting to sound frustrated herself.

"I really can't—"

Tess now stood up too, adding angrily, "If the cruise line's board of directors is trying to cover up what could have become a *mass casualty ev*—"

"The doctor said he had a tiny injection mark in his thigh," Reilly blurted out suddenly, apparently hoping to head off exactly the type of overreaction his supervisors had envisioned.

"*What?!*" Kallie whispered. "Someone just jabbed him in the leg with a needle?" She looked shocked and a little ill at the thought.

Tess quickly moved to Kallie's side and took her hand. "There are cameras everywhere, Kal," she added, comfortingly. "They've probably already caught the guy. Right, officer?"

"We've looked at *hours* of video," the security chief added, sounding defensive. "From a dozen different locations and angles, but we haven't been able to isolate the actual attack yet." He sat back down on the bar stool. "The doctor said the puncture is so small, he might not even have felt it. The hallways and hot spots were jam-packed the first night, and it could have been anyone."

"I need to sit down," Kallie mumbled, collapsing on the couch.

"They aren't coming after us, Kal," Tess sat next to her and pushed her hair out of her face, adding sincerely, "We're safe here."

"Unless we were to start meeting closely and often with the chief of security – so it looked like we were trying to help catch the killer," Kallie whispered back, darkly, trying to mask her growing discomfort.

Officer Reilly shifted awkwardly and stood up again. "Well, we were just talking about your harassing wrong number caller, of course. Nothing more." He opened the door and stepped out into the hallway, turning back as he was about to leave. "We'll look into that angry caller, ladies," he announced, a little louder than necessary, to anyone who might be in earshot. "I'm sure she'd just had a little too much to drink and will be feeling foolish in the morning."

Kallie smiled at his kind attempt to convince any nearby boogiemen that they weren't discussing the murder, but it didn't make her feel much better, in the end.

Chapter Five

Tess and Kallie were sitting in their favorite shady poolside spot the next day, when a noisy kids' birthday party started nearby.

Kallie threw her arm over her face dramatically and groaned at the loud honking and squealing noises coming from the clown, who was apparently a ship employee. When the crowd of children started shrieking, she whined to Tess, "This isn't even the kids' pool, is it? What are they doing here?"

Tess ignored the question and whispered, "Kallie, look," nudging her arm.

Kallie leaned up on her elbows to see what her friend was talking about, and she could see a woman with a pre-teen daughter, sitting on the other side of the party. The woman was crying openly, and another woman was trying to comfort them both. "Well, that's depressing," Kallie replied.

"There's really only one reason for it, though, right? Do you think that's the victim's wife?"

"I doubt it," Kallie answered with a shrug. "I'm sure the wife would be the primary suspect. And even if she was cleared, why would she be down here at the pool?"

"That makes sense," Tess agreed with a nod.

"Just one more person who doesn't realize we're supposed to be having fun," Kallie groused. "She's probably crying because the waffle bar closed at ten."

As the noisy clown finished his act and the children dug into their pizza, suddenly they could hear the sobbing woman's voice. "I can't stand to be in our room, Helen. It's so quiet without him."

"And the concierge can't find us another pair of rooms?" her friend asked, surprised. "The doctor said we could move—"

"The rooms are all full; he said the ship was completely booked." The woman blotted her eyes with a tissue, resignedly. Her daughter – who Kallie guessed was about twelve – was trying to look cool and disinterested, but her eyes and nose were red from crying.

"Maybe we could switch rooms, since I'm in the adjoining suite?"

"That's nice of you, but it would be just as bad. I can smell his shampoo and aftershave everywhere. It's killing me." She started crying again, quietly.

"I'm so sorry, Samantha. What did the police say about finding the killer?" her friend Helen asked, looking around to see if any nosey passengers were listening. Tess and Kallie quickly looked away, guiltily.

Wow, Tess was right after all. What are they doing down here at the pool?

Kallie glanced over at Tess and caught her smirking. She quickly fist-bumped her best friend, and mouthed the words, "Good call."

"There aren't any police on board, just security guards," the victim's wife, Samantha, replied with an annoyed tone. "But they said the killer couldn't have gotten away, so they expect to catch him."

"Couldn't he just steal a lifeboat or something?"

"I thought of that, too. They said the lifeboats are locked up, and they have computerized cameras that constantly scan for jumpers. They said the lifeboats were all searched, though. In case he was just hiding in one of them until we get to the next port." The widow shrugged.

"At least they don't think you did it, Sam," her friend put a hand on her arm.

"Only because Skylar and you and I were in line for late-night ice cream sundaes when it happened." She glanced at her daughter, who was fiddling with her phone and still acting as stoic as only a pre-teen can manage.

"That's lucky."

"It's not *lucky*, Helen. If we'd been with him, he'd probably still be alive," she snapped.

"Not if they really wanted to kill him. They

63

would've just—"

"*Shut up*, Helen!"

Her friend had the decency to look contrite, accepting that she'd said the wrong thing. "I'm glad you're not a suspect, anyway. That would make it even worse."

Samantha nodded but didn't reply, and they sat silently for a while.

Helen went to get them two glasses of white wine, as the afternoon grew hotter, and Sam accepted hers with a sad smile.

"Have you thought of anything else?" Helen asked, gently.

"I can't think of any 'motives,' if that's what you mean. Not even anyone at home, much less someone who would go to the trouble of buying a ticket on the same cruise. I mean, if it's someone local, then why not just do it there?"

Kallie nodded silently in agreement.

"There was one thing," Sam added. "I didn't tell the security guys, but I saw him walk down a hallway on the first floor, toward the engine room that morning. We had been talking about taking a tour of the ship, but Skylar said it was too boring. He sounded disappointed at the time, but he didn't insist on it. And I don't think he scheduled a tour for just himself. So it seemed strange that he was down there – I saw him from the railing."

"You should probably tell them."

"I don't want to get him in trouble, when he was just being his normal, nerdy self," she sighed. "He loved old cars and engines and stuff. I always thought it was so stupid, but now I wish I'd walked down there with him."

Helen nodded silently but kept looking at her friend insistently. "You should tell them," she finally repeated.

"Fine. They said the FBI is boarding the ship when we reach Cozumel, so I'll tell *them* about this stuff, when they get here. These guys aren't even real cops."

They actually are, thank goodness, Kallie thought to herself. *But it's not like we can just walk up and correct her.*

* * * * *

"Okay, you heard all of that, right? I'm not having the world's most annoying dream?" Kallie whispered, as she and Tess made their way back to the room.

"It would be a pretty interesting dream, actually. Way better than the one where you're at the chalkboard in ninth grade geometry and you can't remember any of those formulas," Tess replied. "Probably because it's been twenty years since you even saw a chalkboard."

Kallie nodded. "Okay, that school dream *is* more annoying. But at least no one dies in it. Usually. Why are they talking about her husband's murder by the *pool* of all places?"

"Well, you heard them, they can't get a replacement room. I wouldn't want to be up there either."

"I doubt it's haunted *yet*, Tess."

Tess smacked Kallie with her floppy straw hat and laughed. After a moment, she added, "It must be so lonely and depressing. And besides, Officer Reilly said they aren't going to announce the murder, so apart from a little gossip, no one knows anything. No one's listening to them. Except – you know – *us*."

"And aren't *we* classy?" Kallie added, feeling embarrassed.

"Hey, I thought we were going to solve this, Miss Poirot," Tess pointed out with an arched eyebrow. "We don't have the cred to interview them, so we should be happy to eavesdrop and hopefully save the day."

"I don't know, Tess," Kallie sighed. "Solving the murder was a fun idea when it was just a strange guy in a restaurant. But now that we've seen his grieving wife – and that poor kid trying so hard to be brave – it feels more... personal."

"Hey, Kal. I was just trying to cheer you up." Tess stopped in the middle of the hallway and looked closely at her friend, suddenly serious. "If you don't want to do this, we can just go back to facials and sunscreen and cabana boys. I thought the distraction of playing along might keep you from having those nightmares again."

"You know about the nightmares?" Kallie asked sheepishly.

"Seriously? You've been my best friend since fifth grade. I can literally count how many hours of sleep you're getting by the circles under your eyes."

She poked Kallie on the shoulder with her book, and her best friend looked at her and smiled.

"Maybe we can solve it for Skylar?"

"You bet. Absolutely," Tess agreed.

"And so we can get back to our vacation," Kallie added.

Tess nodded. "Yes. Definitely, we can one hundred percent solve it for that too."

"So what are you going to do with your gift card?" Kallie asked, as they continued toward the elevators.

"I'm not sure," Tess answered. "Everything's covered with our package from the radio station. Even tips and room service."

"Yeah, it's pretty sweet," Kallie answered with a smile. "They have an internet café. You could check your email and stuff."

"Nah, I'm actually kind of enjoying being unplugged."

"After that first day of torture—"

"Exactly," Tess replied with a laugh, then added, "Unless you want to get those pictures of Sherman from your dad?"

"That's okay, we'll be in Cozumel soon. I can survive that long."

"Let's go up to the shopping mall section, then. Maybe we'll find something irresistible." Tess stepped into the elevator and hit the third-floor button, marked 'Shoppes.'

The doors opened a minute later, depositing them into a long hallway full of gift, liquor, and clothing stores.

"Look, there's a candy store," Kallie noted, pointing to one side.

"We have plenty of sugar," Tess laughed. Then she looked to her right and added, "That green bathing suit would be killer on you, though."

"A bikini, Tess?" Kallie groaned. "I hate—"

"It's not really a bikini. I think they call that a tankini. Go try it on," she pushed Kallie toward the doorway, and her friend entered the store, grumbling.

Ten minutes later, Tess had convinced Kallie to take the bathing suit, which wasn't nearly as revealing as one of her own bikinis. Even Kallie had to admit, it looked pretty good, and her old one-piece *was* looking a little faded.

"I don't want to use your gift card from the radio station for—"

Tess handed the tankini to the cashier and insisted, "It's exactly your color, and it fits you perfectly. Discussion ended."

"Thanks, Tess," Kallie answered, blushing. "I *do* really like it."

* * * * *

Tess and Kallie and their new friends met at the rock-climbing wall later that day, since none of them had ever tried it before. Kallie tried the kids' wall first, and found it wasn't quite as difficult as it looked. Tess, with her competitive nature, raced up the harder wall and rang the bell while the rest of them cheered her on.

Before they left, they took adorable selfies in front of the giant orange climbing wall, which Kallie planned to send to her dad as soon as they arrived at a port with Wi-Fi.

"We have facials scheduled for two o'clock," Missy told them. "But do you want to meet for dinner again? Or maybe I can try to get us tickets for the comedy show?"

"That'd be great, I've heard the show's

hilarious," Kallie replied, and Tess nodded agreeably.

"Karaoke after that?" Laura asked with a hopeful grin, but Kallie waved her off.

"Not me. I'll be happy to join in your cheering section, but my singing voice will make your ears bleed. Tess will do it, though."

"I'll need that piña colada first," Tess laughed. "But I'm in, as long as someone sings a duet with me?"

"'Enough is Enough'?" Laura suggested the old disco classic with a challenging smile.

"Oh, see – now you're speaking my language." She looked at Kallie. "You heard her speaking my language."

"I did indeed. But who's doing Streisand and who's doing Summer?" Kallie asked the critical question.

There was no response for a minute, and Missy finally answered, looking at her watch, "You can flip a coin for it, tonight. We have to leave for the spa or we'll be late."

* * * * *

The federal agent boarded the ship by helicopter later that afternoon, before they even reached Cozumel. The large, noisy aircraft seemed tiny compared to the ship, but it was visible on the helipad to everyone around the pool below.

A small crowd gathered, waiting expectantly to see who would exit the helicopter, whispering about rap moguls and corporate heiresses, but they went back to their seats when they saw it was no one famous.

Kallie thought they deserved more than one FBI agent, but apparently a murder at sea wasn't high profile enough to earn a whole team.

But the cavalry has arrived! He'll have this murder solved by dinner time, and then we can hit the island for our snorkeling adventure!

Apparently the agent was also expecting a quick trip and a return flight with someone in custody before the ship even docked in Mexico. But Kallie and Tess could soon hear him arguing angrily with the shipboard security chief.

"I was instructed to pick up the murderer from your brig, Officer Reilly. Are you now telling me that this is impossible?"

"Is there really a *brig*?" Kallie whispered. "Like on Star Trek?"

Tess snorted back a laugh and shushed her. "Shh, I want to hear what they're saying."

The sound of the helicopter's rotors died away, but the wind and the background noise drowned them out for a moment. As they drew closer, though, the men's voices became audible again.

"What do you mean, you don't have the killer in custody?" the federal agent snapped.

"This isn't like the usual deaths, sir," Reilly explained. "The victim's family is all in the clear."

Kallie and Tess looked at each other wide-eyed. *Usual deaths?!* Kallie's face went pale under her sunburn.

"And you haven't found any other suspects?"

"None, sir," Reilly answered. "Not even when we reviewed the security footage."

Kallie could hear the federal agent sigh loudly, even over the sound of the wind.

"Well, that changes our plans," he announced angrily. "*No one* gets off at the port until we resolve this."

"But we can't–"

"That's an order, Officer Reilly. Round up the passengers and crew – *all of them* – in the restaurants, and we'll start interviewing them. I'll requisition some local police to help with crowd control and have our pilot fly them out here. We can't risk allowing the murderer to walk off this ship. Especially on foreign soil."

The security chief nodded. "You'd better come with me, sir. We've got to talk to the captain and the cruise director. Organizing something like this isn't as easy as it sounds."

"Understood, let's go."

Kallie and Tess watched as the men crossed to the main doorway into the ship, and the security chief took out his radio to contact the captain. They quickly disappeared inside – two professional guardians, plotting to catch a killer.

Thank goodness that's settled, Kallie thought to herself, as a sense of relief began replacing her tension and worry.

"Well, I guess we're not getting off the ship this evening, after all," she resignedly added, out loud. She took out her sunblock and started re-applying it, smiling at the sweet coconut smell. "We might as well get comfortable. We could be waiting in worse places."

Tess nodded, putting her feet up and pulling down the brim of her hat. "Star Trek, seriously?"

* * * * *

Kallie and Tess were walking toward the restaurant to meet their friends that evening when a man in black rushed past them, sprinkling confetti and glitter in his wake.

"This place is so weird," Kallie laughed. "Was that a magician?"

"It just looked like a guy in a tux to me," Tess replied, looking quizzically at Kallie. "Was he carrying a hat with a rabbit in it?"

A young blonde woman in a skimpy red dress resembling an ice dancing costume ran past them, chasing after the man. Her kitten heels tapped the floor loudly.

"My bad, that was obviously his assistant, waiting to be sawed in half," Tess corrected herself with a grin. "They must be running late."

Missy joined them outside the restaurant. "I couldn't get tickets for the comedy club tonight, but I got us three tickets for the magician."

Kallie and Tess both laughed, "I think we just saw him!"

"It's apparently a really good act."

"Only three tickets? Where's Laura?"

"She's having dinner with that guy she met on the jogging track." She rolled her eyes. "He's cute, but–"

"The pouty guy? Ick," Tess simply said.

"And if it doesn't work out, she's literally trapped on a boat with him," Kallie agreed.

"She just broke up with a long-term boyfriend, and I think she's still trying to get him out of her head."

"Double ick."

"Well, *you're* staying for dinner with us, my dear," Kallie insisted. "Let's get a table."

"There's nothing open," Missy responded, looking around the crowded room.

"Oh, we've been wanting to sit with strangers, but haven't quite been brave enough yet," Kallie answered. "Who should we pick?"

"Strangers?" Missy asked, confused.

"It's apparently a traditional cruise ship activity," Tess explained, looking around the dining room at their options. "You can ask to be placed at any table with open seats, but I think we'd better choose for ourselves."

"At least the first time," Kallie agreed. "There are some young women over there who look nice."

Tess moved over a few steps for a better view and answered, "They have a baby in a high chair."

"Oh, no thanks," Kallie laughed. "I like this dress too much to have it shellacked in mashed potatoes."

Kallie and Tess had both been hesitant at the idea of sitting at the same table with strangers at dinner, when the subject was first mentioned, but it suddenly seemed like an adventure.

"No one on this side looks like they're having any fun," Missy pointed out. "I don't want to sit with people who're in a bad mood."

"Neither do we," Tess answered. "Let's check the other side."

Moving to the other side of the entrance doors, they immediately noticed a cute older couple who were laughing together. They seemed cheerful and definitely in love, but not overly amorous – the girls didn't want to interrupt a romance in bloom.

"What about those two?" Missy asked.

"Absolutely," Tess answered.

"They're adorable," Kallie added with a grin.

"Excuse us," Tess interjected, with her usual endearing grace. "We were interested in trying this table-sharing thing. Do you mind if we sit with you?"

The couple both burst into huge smiles and moved their chairs to the side. "We'd love that! Come on, sit down!"

Kallie, Tess, and Missy slid into the open seats and thanked the friendly couple.

"I'm Michael and this is my wife Megan," the husband introduced them in a heavy New York accent. "This is our first cruise."

"But not our last," his wife replied with a laugh. "And I know it's the popular cliché, but it feels like we're seeing each other with fresh eyes. This is the first time we've both been able to play hooky from work and put our phones down in six months."

"It's amazing, right?" Kallie agreed, and added jokingly, "After the initial shock and withdrawal symptoms?" She wasn't glued to her phone, even at home, but she knew Tess was still adjusting.

"We're from Florida, and Missy is from Georgia," Tess said. "It sounds like you're from New York?"

"Albany," Megan answered.

"My sister's on the cruise with me, but she's on a date," Missy explained.

"Oh, that's awkward," Megan replied, looking startled at her own bluntness when they all laughed.

"That's what *we* said!" Tess replied.

"Dating is so perilous, even on dry land. I'd expect all of the men on the ship to be secretly married and cheating on their wives."

"Ugh, I didn't even think about that possibility," Missy replied, shaking her head.

"I did that one time, remember?" Michael reminded his wife, who chuckled and elbowed him in the ribs.

Their three dinner guests looked at them curiously, and Megan relented, telling the story.

"I caught my husband out to lunch, at my favorite restaurant, in a cozy little candlelit booth with my sister."

"*Michael?!* You didn't." Tess gasped, already feeling comfortable with this cute couple.

Michael blushed but remained silent.

"I wasn't sure exactly what to say, I was so shocked," Megan answered. "Not as shocked as he was, though. He jumped up, sat back down, shoved some papers into my sister's purse, and then started shouting 'It's not what it looks like!' My sister watched him freak out for a minute, then just sat back shaking her head."

Tess looked at Michael for his reply, but he wasn't talking.

"He tried insisting that they were meeting to talk about the district changes at school – both of our kids were attending the same elementary school at the time – and then said she needed help with her car. It was embarrassing to watch. I felt like I was going to vomit, but even then he looked like such an idiot."

"And what about your sister?" Tess asked.

Megan laughed. "I was about ready to start screaming at both of them right there in the middle of the restaurant, when she said, 'Shut up, Michael. It's not worth it.' She took out the wrinkled papers that he'd shoved into her purse, spread them out on the table, and said, 'We're planning a surprise party for your fortieth. You might as well sit down and help us."

Kallie laughed too. "Now *that's* awkward!"

"Seriously," Megan nodded.

"Was she telling the truth?" Missy asked.

"Yep. I wasn't convinced, but I grabbed the papers for a look, and they had rented out the big party room at Weeki Wachee on my birthday. They even got me lessons with the performers. He knows how much I love mermaids."

"She's crazy about mermaids," he agreed. "We were planning airfare to Florida and hotel stays, and of course booking the party itself at the state park – plus arranging the time off from work for all of us – all while trying to keep it a secret. It took a lot of organization, and her sister is a great planner."

Tess shook her head in mock disapproval at Michael, while stifling a laugh. "Tsk, tsk."

"I didn't really *lie*; I just didn't have an excuse planned for if she caught us." He turned to his wife, "Thank goodness your sister has more sense than I do. I didn't even think about how it must look, until you were standing right there!"

"I still hate that it ruined the surprise," Megan sighed. "It really was a great plan."

"Yeah, but like she said, it wouldn't be much of a party if you divorced me before your birthday."

"This is true."

* * * * *

After dinner and goodbyes to their adorable tablemates, Kallie, Tess, and Missy hurried to another floor in time to catch the magic act.

"Oh my gosh, it's freezing in here," Kallie

complained as they dropped into their seats by the stage.

"I know, I wish I'd brought a cardigan," Missy agreed.

"Do you think we have time to run back and get them from the room?"

"No, I think the show's starting—"

As they were talking, the room went completely black, as if the power had gone out. A pop of flame suddenly appeared on the dark stage, and then a scantily clad woman spun into view. When she reached the center, another batch of fireballs burst into light around her. The sequins on her tiny red dress and heels reflected the flames and made her look like a phoenix for a moment.

Suddenly a bolt of ashy grey fabric unspooled from the ceiling, wrapping the twirling young woman like a movie mummy. She struggled gracefully, arms and legs twisting, until the handsome magician darted from the other side of the stage. Rushing to her side, he held up one hand, and a final blast of fire appeared on his palm.

At the same moment, the woman vanished, her wrappings falling limply to the floor.

The stunned audience sat silent for a moment and then burst into applause.

"Wow, that was some entrance," Tess whispered.

Kallie nodded in agreement, clapping happily with the rest of the crowd, when the room went dark again. They waited a moment for the act to continue, but the small theater stayed enveloped in blackness. Kallie's skin started to crawl as the darkness seemed to close in around her.

Come on.

Lights, please.

Kallie felt her heart start to pound, as fear threatened to overwhelm her.

Why did we even come here? There's a killer on the ship, and we're watching a magician? In the dark? Like fish in a barrel?

She tried to peer into the darkness of the room but could barely even make out shadows.

Is that a shape coming toward us? Wouldn't this be the perfect spot to murder someone? The audience would think it's part of the act.

Don't panic, Kalliope. You can—

A bright yellow spotlight suddenly lit up a wooden box onstage, with a hinged door, holding the lovely assistant. The magician began clanging a few swords against the wood.

Kallie sighed and relaxed her tensed muscles, slumping against the back of her chair. While everyone else clapped, she tried to slow her racing heart.

"The history of sword tricks goes back hundreds

of years, but we're willing to bet you've never seen one quite like this," the magician announced, as he closed the door of the box – leaving only the assistant's face showing.

"You okay, Kal?" Tess whispered.

"Sure," Kallie answered, settling back down for the show. "Just fine."

* * * * *

"Are we still going to karaoke even though Laura's not here?" Kallie asked, after the magician's act finished, and they made their way to the lounge. "It was her idea."

"I told her the magic show ended at ten o'clock, and she said she'd meet us there."

"Is she usually on time for things?"

"Not really," Missy replied with a crooked smile. "But it's karaoke. That's pretty high on her priority list."

They soon sat at a high table in the most popular lounge, and ordered drinks while Tess flipped through the song list looking for the perfect tune. It was a huge list, in a notebook binder, but at least it was categorized. Kallie and Missy looked over Tess's shoulder and pointed out their favorite songs. Finally she found the one she wanted and added her name to the list.

"It's almost eleven, and Laura's still not here.

Are you sure she's coming?"

"Hopefully this means her date's going well, but she wouldn't skip out on us," Missy replied. "I'm sure she'll be here."

Tess saw her name pop up on the screen and took a deep breath. She started to walk up to the stage for her turn, then grabbed one more sip from her piña colada for bravery. Kallie clapped as she climbed onto the stage.

They went to karaoke in Owhiro occasionally, but that was always the same crowd. This was a whole new group of people about to hear her best friend sing. Apart from being gorgeous and brilliant, Tess was also a killer singer. If Kallie didn't love her so much, she'd be easy to hate.

Since Laura hadn't shown up for their duet, Tess was singing a song by herself – the Etta James version of 'These Foolish Things'.

Through the intro, Kallie could see that no one was paying attention, chatting and sipping their drinks, but it got quiet when she started singing and her sultry, cool voice hit them. When she came to the line about the winds of March making her heart a dancer, Kallie got instant goosebumps, and she heard several people in the crowd whisper, "Wow."

When she finished, they all cheered, and Tess bowed playfully with a laugh before jumping off the stage.

She was visibly cheered up to see Laura at their table, apologizing to everyone for being late.

"Hey, good to see you, sunshine. How was your date?" Tess asked her, with a hug.

"Ugh, don't ask," Laura replied with a grimace.

"That bad?"

"I don't even know where to start. How about when he called the sushi chef a name that would've made my grandfather blush? Or when he started a fight with the wine guru at the restaurant?"

"Oh, honey," Missy sighed.

"This is exactly why I'm not making eye contact with any men on board," Tess replied, shaking her head.

"He yelled at the sommelier?" Kallie asked.

"No, he actually picked a fight. He tried to punch the guy."

"*What?!*"

"And he prefers 'wine guru,' by the way. He says it's less stuffy. Luckily, his defensive skills are just as good as his dinner pairings. He sent the jerk running."

"I'm so sorry."

"That part was a sight to behold, actually. Almost worth the rest of the awful evening. I should've known it was a bad idea to go out with someone I met at a gym. Especially a cruise gym."

"So are you going to have to hide from that jerk

the whole rest of the cruise?" Kallie asked.

"I hope not. Security said they'd keep an eye on him. Anyway, I'm meeting the wine guru for pizza tomorrow night, and I know he can keep me safe," she added with a laugh.

"Girlfriend, I don't know if you're crazy or inspiring," Tess smiled. "After a date like that, I'd avoid the whole male half of the species for months."

Laura held out a photo on her phone and they grudgingly agreed that the 'wine guru' was awfully cute. Then she asked if it was too late for their duet – just as a waiter delivered a drink to Tess from a new fan.

"We'll have to get back in the queue, but there should be plenty of time," Tess replied, as a middle-aged dad started a pretty great cover of 'Heartbreak Hotel' on stage, to the crowd's delight. "Are we really doing 'Enough Is Enough', or were you kidding? I can go sign us up."

She teasingly reached toward the signup sheet, as she let Laura decide.

"Okay, but you're definitely doing the Streisand part, after hearing you sing."

"You got it! You can be the incredible Donna Summer."

Kallie ordered a huge plate of nachos for them all, while Tess went to sign them up for the song.

"Have you heard anything else about the

murder," Missy asked, surprising Kallie.

Not wanting to admit how much they'd overheard, Kallie answered, "Not really. We saw the FBI land in a helicopter, though. So I'm sure it'll all be over soon. Try not to worry too much."

"Corey said they can't let us off the ship until the interviews are done," Laura added, sipping her drink.

"Huh? Who's Corey?" her sister asked, confused.

"The wine guru," Laura answered with a wistful smile. "He said the ship isn't leaving Cozumel, and we're all being interviewed by the FBI. Staff and passengers, everyone."

"Would a wine guru really know all that?" Missy wondered aloud.

"If the ship isn't leaving, it makes sense that the whole crew and staff would need to know," Tess answered, sitting back down. "It means we'll miss the stop in Montego Bay, and they'll have to rearrange their schedules."

Someone started singing 'Margaritaville' on the stage, and they all paused to sing along with the chorus.

"Did your handsome wine guru say anything else?" Tess asked when the song ended.

"Just that I have lovely eyes," Laura answered with a laugh, fluttering her lashes. "He didn't even know about the murder until they cancelled the stop in

Jamaica."

"Then I guess we'll just have to wait for the interviews, and hope the FBI finds their killer before our whole vacation is scrubbed," Kallie answered with a sigh.

An '80s power ballad soon ended behind them, garnering some scattered applause, and the digital screens updated with a new list of names.

"We're up next!" Tess cheered excitedly, and their strange vacation seemed better immediately.

Chapter Six

"I want a Cuban, Tess," Kallie mumbled from under her pillow.

"What? You're thinking about lunch already?" Her best friend rolled over to look at the clock. "It's not even six a.m."

"It would be fine for breakfast too."

"I don't think you want to try it on the cruise. Let's just wait until we get home."

"I *caaan't–*" Kallie whined pitifully, making Tess laugh. Cuban sandwiches were hugely popular where they lived near Tampa, but they required Cuban bread and needed to be cooked in a special press.

"They won't have the right bread. They'll probably make it on Wonder Bread and stick it in the microwave."

"I like Wonder Bread–"

"You wouldn't like it in a Cuban, Kal."

"Okay..." she mumbled, still half asleep.

"What about a Reuben?" Tess suggested, trying to be helpful. "I saw that on the menu at the Deli."

"Just because it rhymes with Cuban doesn't make it the same—"

"You goofball!" Tess laughed out loud and threw her spare pillow at Kallie's bed.

"I don't like rye bread."

"I don't either, but they can make it on sourdough or something. Go back to sleep, and we can think about lunch later."

"Are we going to catch the killer, Tess?"

"You bet we are, Kal. Absolutely."

But she was already asleep.

* * * * *

Kallie and Tess stood in line at their favorite kiosk later, watching the couple in front of them get green drinks – kale-based with spinach, wheat grass, and pineapple. They looked at each other and shrugged. *No accounting for taste.*

"Make mine a strawberry and banana, please," Kallie asked, when it was their turn. "No offense, but that looked way too healthy."

"It's not that bad, as long as the stems are all trimmed off," their barista friend replied with a smile. "The pineapple juice sweetens it up."

"I'll take pineapple and mango, then," Tess

replied. She jokingly added, "All of the sweet and none of the green."

"One pineapple and mango, coming up."

Kallie looked around to make sure no one was in earshot. "How's your husband? Did the security people interview him?"

"You heard about that?" the barista replied with surprise. "They interviewed both of us – but we were both on the clock, and on the wrong floor to be guilty or see anything. What about you? It must be awful, having your vacation spoiled."

"It's definitely not what we expected, but it hasn't spoiled our trip yet," Kallie answered. "They sounded pretty confident about finding the guy. Hopefully the killer will confess, and they'll let us off in Cozumel."

"I doubt we'll make it to Cozumel," Tess added, unhappily. "We were scheduled to leave for Jamaica today, and we still need to talk to the federal agent. But maybe they'll let us off in Grand Cayman at least, before we have to go back."

"I hope they find him soon," the barista sighed. "I don't like the idea of a killer running loose on the ship. I'm sure it sounds silly, with all of the tourists and security guards and cameras, but this is our home. My husband said–"

She stopped and looked around cautiously. Kallie and Tess both nodded for her to go on.

She stayed silent as she handed over Kallie's drink, then quietly added, "I don't want to worry you, but my husband thinks the killer could just be hiding. That he wouldn't even need to get off the ship when we get back to Tampa, and he could just keep sailing with us on the next trip."

"Whoa." Kallie felt a chill run up her spine at the thought.

"It scares me a little," the barista added, softly.

Wow, that scares me a lot, and I don't even live here, Kallie thought to herself.

"Well, they have the whole passenger manifest. I'm sure they're verifying that everyone is found and interviewed," Tess reassured her.

"And if there's anyone on the list who they can't find, and who might be hiding, they'd start a search right away," Kallie added. "Try not to worry too much."

"I'm sure you're right," the barista answered nervously. "Now I'm just scaring myself. I'm Daphne, by the way – thank you for talking to me about all this. My husband says I shouldn't be scared, and then he tells me something scary." She laughed shakily.

"I'm Kallie and this is my best friend Tess, and we're happy if we helped at all." She reached across the counter, standing on tiptoe, and hugged the young lady. "Your husband's right, you shouldn't be scared. I'm sure no one else is in danger."

"I hope you're right," Daphne replied.

Me too, Kallie thought to herself.

* * * * *

"Can I help you ladies with anything?" a young, freckled deck aide asked, trying to sound smooth while stumbling clumsily over a lounge chair to get near Tess. Kallie wondered if this was his first week working on a cruise ship.

Tess could be sarcastic and quick-witted, but she was also gorgeous – and Kallie had watched many otherwise cocky guys absentmindedly walk into walls, or dump salt in their coffee, while talking to her.

This poor bonehead never stood a chance.

"Do you think you could find us a seat near those cute flamingo statues?" Tess asked, not mentioning their real intention. "We'd love to get–"

She didn't need to finish her made-up excuse, because the kid was off like a shot. "Of course, it'd be my pleasure," he yelped, tripping over the lounge chair again.

"The flamingo statues?" Kallie asked, with a crooked smile.

"Well, I couldn't really ask for a nice, shady seat near the bereaved, where we can effortlessly eavesdrop on their private conversation, could I?"

"I'm pretty sure you could've, actually," Kallie

answered with a chuckle, watching the deck aide galloping around the poolside. "He probably would've dropped a microphone in Samantha's purse for you, if you batted your eyelashes."

Soon he was wildly shoving chairs and tables around to make a brand-new space for them, marking it occupied, and escorting them to their new seats. They now found themselves barely ten feet away from Samantha and Skylar.

Tess thanked him sweetly while he practically drooled on his shoes.

"I can't believe they're still out here in the open," Kallie whispered once they were alone again. She felt a bit guilty about eavesdropping, but her main feeling was still shock, mixed with mild dismay, that the little group was lounging by the pool when their family member had just been killed.

No one else seemed to care, or even recognize them, though.

"I really don't think anyone knows about the murder," Tess reasoned. "There hasn't been an announcement or anything, and Officer Reilly said they only went door-to-door to meet the people they identified in the hallway. And he didn't even mention that it was a murder until you asked."

"It still looks unseemly," Kallie replied. "I'd be in my room, sobbing."

"Yeah, me too. But everyone grieves differently.

And maybe they just weren't that cute, lovestruck, happy couple, you know?"

"I guess…" Kallie replied, unconvinced.

"Oh, here comes her friend," Tess hissed quietly. "Shh."

They both bent strategically over their books, while still listening intently.

"Hey, hon." The woman they knew only as Helen hugged the young widow and her daughter. "Hi Skylar. It didn't sound like you two were awake when I left the room this morning. How are you holding up?"

Skylar didn't look up from her tablet, where she was apparently playing a game, but her mother made space for her friend to sit down.

"How do you think?" Samantha asked, but she didn't sound sarcastic, just tired and sad.

"Did you get any sleep?"

"A little. The ship's doctor gave me a sedative, but it didn't do much."

Kallie tried not to look, but she'd already noticed that the widow appeared exhausted, like she hadn't slept in weeks. Even with quite a bit of makeup, the tears and insomnia left dark circles under her eyes.

"Have the security guys told you anything else?" Helen asked, pulling a bottle of sunscreen out of her bag. "I heard the FBI arrived yesterday in a helicopter."

"They really haven't told me anything. I guess

it's for the best, though. Once they figured out that I couldn't have killed him, they started focusing on everyone else."

"They should at least keep you informed," Helen insisted.

"Yeah, I'd like an update or two," Sam agreed, "But I'm glad they seem to be really invested in finding out who did it. We'll be gone in a few days. They could've just put on a big show for the tourists' cameras, until we leave and stop complicating their lives."

The jaded tone of the widow's voice made Kallie cringe, but she was glad Reilly was actively working on the case too.

"Did you tell the police that he had an affair?" her friend asked.

An affair?

Tess and Kallie looked at each other for a second, eyes wide, wishing they could talk – but they were sitting too close. They quickly looked back at their books.

"They aren't the police, they're just security officers," Sam explained impatiently again. "And no, I didn't tell them. It was a long time ago, and it's none of their business."

"Sam, if it comes out later, it'll look like–"

"How could this possibly be related to his affair?" the widow argued. "That was almost five years ago, and the bimbo went back to her husband. We had long since reconciled."

"I just think—"

"It's not like I was an angel at the time, either. We were both working too much, and never saw each other," she paused for a moment. "We didn't like each other very much, frankly. When we did see each other, we were usually fighting. It's not like that anymore."

After a moment she corrected herself with a sigh, "*Wasn't* like that anymore."

"Are you sure?"

Kallie noticed that *Helen* definitely didn't sound sure.

"That we were good? Yes, I'm sure."

"Because, I mean, we know there was one angry husband with a grudge out there. Maybe there were more. Are you sure he wasn't still—?"

"Helen, *yes*. There was no one else after that one affair," Sam insisted, adding quietly, "I let him know what would happen if he ever did it again."

"Sensible," Helen replied, obviously impressed. "But even if he was faithful in the end, there might have been others in the past. The cops need to check to see if any of them were maybe blackmailing him? Or stalking him? Or their husbands finally acted on their belated jealousy?"

"Okay, okay. Stop talking about it," the widow

sighed. "I'll tell them so they can check. Discreetly."

"Thank you," Helen answered with a gentle smile. "I'm going to get a mojito. Do you want anything?"

"Yes, but I'll get it." Samantha stood up and stretched. "I've been sitting down for too long, and I'll get this round. Skylar, do you want another lemonade?"

The young girl nodded without looking up from her tablet.

Helen watched her friend walk away and sighed audibly at her obvious sadness. Kallie felt the same way.

* * * * *

"Hey, babe. How's it going?"

Kallie cringed at the lame pick-up line, thinking it was someone flirting with Tess – but when she looked up, she saw that it was a strange man, talking to the widow's friend. She expected Helen to chase him away, but instead she looked cautiously over her shoulder, apparently to see if Samantha was watching.

Surely she's not having an onboard fling! Her best friend's husband was murdered barely forty-eight hours ago!

"Pete, I can't talk to you right now." She jumped up and pulled him away from their seats. "Can't you see that I'm trying to take care of my friend? We've had a *tragedy* in the family, in case you hadn't heard."

Tess and Kallie looked at each other, bemused by the way she'd hissed the word 'tragedy' – like she was acting in her own personal soap opera.

"Hey, that's okay, babe," her apparent beau replied coolly, his shoulder-length hair blowing around his upturned collar. "We don't need to talk now. You can meet me at the frozen yogurt place again tonight."

Helen looked like she wanted to say no, glancing back at the empty seat next to her own, but then nodded silently. "Later, though. Eleven."

"You got it, babe. I'll be waiting."

If he said 'babe' one more time, Kallie thought she'd puke on her shoes. *Could this guy sound any more like a stoned loser? And that mullet.* She couldn't imagine what Helen saw in him. Kallie reminded herself again that everyone handled grief differently, and wondered if this was part of it.

"Want to get fresh drinks, *babe*?" Tess asked her quietly, with a giggle.

"I'll go get them, babe. And maybe a frozen yogurt."

"I love frozen yogurt, babe."

Kallie picked up their glasses and walked to the bar, still chuckling, but trying to keep it quiet out of respect for the widow. If that goof wasn't a shipboard hookup, then who was he? Someone Helen knew from home? Or had she been desperate for somewhere else to sleep, weary of listening to her friend cry?

"Two more sweet iced teas, please," Kallie asked at the counter, still curious about the unlikely couple, and wondering if Tess wanted to get 'fro-yo' at eleven o'clock.

* * * * *

"Oh, look," Kallie said as they got off the elevator on their own floor later. She gestured toward a small table near the entrance to their wing of the ship. "Someone left their magazines." There was a handwritten note on top of the glossy, celebrity-strewn magazines that said: *Help yourself.*

"Hey, it's like the world's trashiest Little Free Library," Tess replied with a smirk, following Kallie to check it out.

"That's really nice, isn't it? I mean, there's no need to keep them after you've finished reading them." There were a few more tasteful magazines in the stack, showing gardening trends and the latest popular paint colors, but most of them specialized in paparazzi photos and bickering starlets.

"I'm surprised the ship allows this, actually," Tess commented, checking out the offerings. "It's cutting down on their sales, right?"

"I'll go get the tabloids I've already read," Kallie replied. "I haven't seen these issues yet." She wasn't really the type to read gossip magazines at home, but it was a guilty pleasure while on vacation.

"I wouldn't mind reading this one," Tess agreed, pulling out a cooking magazine from the bottom of the pile. "I'll come with you."

They quickly returned from their room with a few magazines, adding them to the display – both feeling a little embarrassed – and took a few in exchange.

"Heiress elopes with paparazzi photographer?" Tess read one of the cover headlines with a laugh, as they walked back toward their suite with the new additions. "I think that editor's dreaming."

"It won't win the Pulitzer Prize, but it's—"

Suddenly, they heard a loud commotion in one of the rooms behind them.

"She doesn't have to answer questions from you," a young voice yelled angrily. "My father just DIED!"

Kallie and Tess looked at each other, startled, and turned hesitantly back toward the sound.

"Was that Skylar?" Tess whispered.

"It sounded like her," Kallie replied, looking worried. "And she's probably the only kid on board whose family is rich enough to stay up here in the suites."

"I'm sorry, young lady," a woman's tense voice replied, "but we need to ask–"

"You're so rude!" the girl continued, now near hysterics. "I can't believe you're bothering her right now."

They heard the widow's friend, Helen, intervene gently. "They need this information to catch your dad's killer, Skylar. She doesn't mean to be rude." Their footsteps tapped away, into another room.

"Thank you," Samantha's voice called out, though they were already gone. The victim's wife sounded so small then, all alone, without even her daughter to protect her.

Kallie and Tess leaned against the wall, out of sight but listening closely.

"When was the last time you saw your husband?" they heard the security chief ask the widow, apparently continuing a previous discussion from before the outburst.

The bereaved woman sighed audibly, "It was about nine o'clock, I think," she answered. "He was joining a conference call with his partners at the office about some big case."

"I see," they heard a woman answer, whose voice they recognized as Officer Carol Navarro, trailing off to encourage the widow to continue.

"I was upset because he'd promised he wouldn't work while we were on the cruise," she added sadly, barely audible. "I can show you where we were." The chair squeaked as she stood up, possibly to lead the security members to another location.

"It's okay, you can show us after we finish talking, Mrs. Devin."

Kallie and Tess heard the chair squeak again, as Samantha sat back down without replying.

"I'm sorry to ask you this," Navarro continued. "But do you know of anyone who would've wanted to hurt your husband?"

"He was a lawyer—" the new widow answered, quietly. "He sued a lot of companies and forced some of them out of business – so he had some enemies. But not on a ship," she added, her voice pleading. "They wouldn't be on a cruise ship, right?"

Kallie suddenly gasped quietly, and her eyes widened in surprise.

"Tess, that's—" she started to say, but Tess shushed her, a little impatiently. They couldn't afford to get caught eavesdropping, especially right now.

"We'll need a list of those people as soon as you can put one together," Reilly advised her. "We can get you a satellite phone if you need to call his office to get the names."

Navarro added consolingly, "It's unlikely that one of them would be on the ship, but we need to check."

"He'd just die if he ran into one of those defendants out here," she explained, and then realized what she'd said and started crying again.

After she calmed down a few minutes later, the female investigator asked, "Were you having any marital or family issues?"

"No, we were all just at Sundae Fundae, getting ice cream. He was going to join–"

"That's not what I mean, ma'am. Not having issues that night, but in general. We need to know if there's anyone who–"

There was silence for a moment and then they heard the widow sniff angrily as she processed the question. "A jilted ex-lover?" she snapped. "Of course not!"

Wait, didn't she promise Helen that she would tell Reilly about the affair? It's going to look bad for her, when he inevitably finds out about it later. She obviously doesn't trust Reilly, but I wonder why?

They all sat in an uncomfortable silence for a minute or two, which Kallie suspected Reilly had engineered to keep her talking.

"He was a good man. He might have been a little... *ruthless* in his job," she finally sighed. "But he was a good husband and a great dad. He taught Skylar to play the guitar, and practiced lacrosse with her. Everyone only sees him as this cutthroat, rich lawyer, but there was more to him..."

She trailed off, and they sat in silence again.

"Understood," Reilly finally replied. "And were you having any money problems, Mrs. Devin?"

"Nothing serious. Skylar's school is expensive, and she'll want a car soon." She sighed. "It's not that we can't afford it, but it causes some stress."

Did she hesitate at that question? Kallie wondered to herself.

One of the investigators responded, "Mmm-hmm." Kallie couldn't tell which of them.

"But nothing that he'd be killed over," Sam added.

The questioning ended and the investigators thanked her – a sign for Kallie and Tess to make a rapid retreat. As they moved quickly down the hallway from the Devins' suite, they heard Skylar immediately run back to her mother, who started crying again.

When they'd turned the last corner before their room, Kallie finally stopped and excitedly grabbed her friend. "Reilly just called her 'Mrs. Devin,' Tess! *That's* why he was killed. It must be!"

Tess shook her head and looked confused.

"Her husband's the 'Sue the Bozo' guy!"

"I think you spent too much time in the sun today," Tess replied with a laugh. She unlocked their suite door and they sat down on the couch.

"Haven't you seen those billboards and commercials? You know, 'Don't suffer solo, sue the bozo'," Kallie sang the jingle.

"Oh my gosh, the 1-800-SUE-BOZO guy?" Tess answered. "I didn't know his real name. *That's* who the murder victim was?"

"Rex Devin! I saw him on the news during the last election, pushing some tax proposition. I'd forgotten his name too, until she said he was a lawyer!"

"Winchester *hates* those guys," Tess replied with a frown, considering this new information. Her boss was an elderly and very honest attorney, who didn't hold back on his opinions. "They claim to only take money from insurance companies in their massive lawsuits, but if a company can't get re-insured, they're out of business. Which is fine, if the company is really guilty – but Winchester says they're creating a fraud tidal wave."

"It sounds like your boss isn't the only one who hates them. If Devin was destroying companies in court, that *must* be why he was killed, right?"

"It makes more sense than anything else we've heard so far," Tess nodded, deep in thought about this new development. "Ugh, I wish the ship's internet access wasn't so expensive, so I could look up his recent cases."

Kallie asked, "You follow all of those crime bloggers. Do you think he filed some fraudulent injury case and the defendant came out here and killed him?"

"It's not impossible. Winchester is the best kind of attorney, and even he has a few enemies," Tess replied. After a little more thought, she added, "But if we're speculating wildly about random outsiders boarding cruise ships to commit murder, then anyone could've done it. Even the widow could just as easily have sent a hired killer."

"Oh, you're right," Kallie sighed.

"But it wouldn't be the first time a lawyer was killed by an angry defendant, and there are weirder ways to kill someone than to trap them on a cruise ship," Tess added. "I'd love to see the widow's enemies list, though – I'll bet it's a doozy."

Chapter Seven

Kallie and Tess sat down in their prime spying seats by the pool that afternoon just in time to hear the widow hiss snappishly at her friend, "Helen, you can't keep running off with that guy. Even if it's just to the frozen yogurt stand."

Wow, Kallie thought to herself, still empathetic, but also slightly appalled, *she really doesn't have any sense of subtlety at all. Who talks about this kind of thing by the pool?*

"What?" her friend replied, obviously thinking she'd been subtle. "With Pete? Why not?"

"Well, because you're married, for one thing. And people will talk."

"None of these people know us, Samantha," Helen sighed. "Who do you think they'll tell?"

"It's an awfully small world," the widow replied, sounding weary. "And my husband was just murdered, in case you hadn't noticed. If you won't pretend to care about appearances for my sake, then at least consider how many people will be putting photos of us on social media, if we ever get off this ship."

"So what?" Helen asked, sounding genuinely confused.

Confused and naïve, Kallie thought.

"So, one of them will catch that guy in a photo with you. People love to gossip, and we're becoming the prime story around here."

"My husband didn't want to come with us because he gets seasick – in case you forgot."

"And if he sees you on social media with some blonde gigolo with a mullet, he'll never go anywhere with us, *ever* again," her friend concluded.

Helen paled at the thought and answered awkwardly, "There's nothing going on between me and Pete. But I understand your point."

"You expect me to believe there's nothing going on?" Samantha smirked. "I've seen you two canoodling."

"Sorry? Canoodling?"

Tess looked at Kallie and mouthed the word, "*Canoodling?*"

"You know exactly what I mean, Helen."

"It's not... I don't want to talk about it." Helen dropped the subject, and her friend seemed to think her point was sufficiently made. She let it go.

Helen and Pete had seemed like a romantic pair to Tess and Kallie too, although they had seen much worse on this trip. People could be pretty public about their affection, and many of them apparently thought they were invisible.

Kallie blamed the fresh sea air and a mega-dose of cabin fever.

* * * * *

That evening, seated at their own table for dinner this time, Kallie sipped her drink and commented, "I hope this fettuccini primavera is huge. I'm starving."

"Me too," Tess replied. "Did we burn a lot of calories today or something? I feel like I haven't eaten in a week."

The waitress brought their dishes, which were indeed enormous, and they dug in happily.

"Did you know a crab has more legs than an octopus?" a cheerful voice called from the next table, as a waitress passed with a tray of shellfish.

"Freddy, shush," his wife whispered.

Kallie was suddenly glad she hadn't ordered seafood tonight.

"Crabs have ten legs, and an octopus only has eight," he added merrily.

"Freddy, they don't care."

"And they have taste buds on their feet," he

added.

Kallie immediately pictured a crab wearing five pairs of her brother's stinky old gym shoes and looked away, stifling a laugh. His wife must have mistaken it for annoyance, or possibly gagging, because she started apologizing profusely.

"I'm so sorry. My husband thinks everyone shares his interest in random, useless trivia." She nudged his shoulder and whispered loudly, "Leave these poor women alone. They're trying to finish their dinner."

Kallie sipped her strawberry lemonade as the couple argued quietly for a moment and then fell silent.

"I reserved our spa visit for tomorrow morning," Tess said after they'd made a significant dent in their meals. "We're scheduled for ten o'clock."

"Oh, I forgot that was included in the prize. That'll be nice."

"I think it's just a massage and a facial."

"Do you know how long it's been since I had a massage?" Kallie twirled her fettuccini, adding, "And I've never had a professional facial. Although, to be honest, I've never really wanted one."

"It sounds a little creepy to me too," Tess replied with a laugh. "I'm sure it's not as much like 'some total stranger touching your face' as it sounds."

Kallie covered a laugh with her napkin. "But it's

still going to be fun. This whole thing has been amazing, regardless of the other gruesome weirdness. I'm so glad we're here."

"Me too. I saw a sign that they're having afternoon tea tomorrow. Let's go to that, okay?" Tess asked.

"Cucumber finger sandwiches and scones? I'm in."

"Excellent, my dear," Tess replied, toasting with her diet coke, pinkie outstretched.

"I always thought it was so boring when my mother wanted to go for afternoon tea in South Tampa, and then spent the whole time telling me to be quiet," Kallie commented. "It'll be way more fun with you."

"I promise not to tell you to be quiet, unless you start spouting trivia about jellyfish or something."

"I'll try to refrain," Kallie answered with a smile.

They finished their dinner and prepared to leave the dining room, waving good night politely to the couple next to them.

"Did you know fish have nostrils?" Freddy called after them, louder than his wife's annoyed groan. "So they can smell things, even though they have gills to breathe."

"Okay, that's actually interesting," Kallie whispered to Tess as they walked quickly out the door.

* * * * *

Sitting in the warm sun beside a glorious pool, while lazily watching the ocean drift past, was lovely. For a few days. But by the next morning, Kallie decided she'd had enough.

"I know this sounds insane, but I'm actually getting bored with just sitting by the pool."

"That *does* sound insane," Tess replied without opening her eyes.

"Don't you want to find something else to do?"

Tess smiled and grabbed her floppy hat from the side table. "Sure, we can do something. The announcement board said that the federal agent is interviewing the staff today, so I'm sure our massages and the afternoon tea will both be cancelled."

"Oh, that figures," Kallie replied with a pout.

"Anyway, we have sun and pools in Owhiro, too, as I recall. So what did you have in mind?"

"I want to ride the roller coaster and take the ship tour," Kallie immediately answered. "I heard there's a ghost tour, too."

"A ghost tour? Tess asked, incredulously. "How old is this ship?"

And how many people have died? Kallie mused for a moment.

"I'm not sure. Old enough to have a bunch of

ghosts, apparently. But that suddenly sounds less exciting and more depressing. The regular tour is supposed to be good, though. The brochure said the focus is on the places passengers never see."

"That sounds cool. I'll bet there are a ton of interesting stories," Tess replied cheerfully. "Hey, do you think that's the tour that the victim wanted to take, before his daughter put the kibosh on it? The widow said he wanted to see the engines."

"Those are the only two tours I saw on the list, so I guess that must be the one."

"Let's sign up for that," Tess agreed. "And I'll go on the roller coaster with you, if you'll go on the ropes course with me."

"That's a deal," Kallie agreed. "Although I don't promise to be any good at it."

Tess pulled out her phone, which she had barely used, from her poolside bag and handed it over. "I have the ship's scheduling app on my phone, so you can sign us up for the tour from here. See if anything else looks interesting."

Kallie took the phone and quickly signed them up for the one o'clock tour. "There's no sign-up for the roller coaster, but I booked us a time this afternoon for the ropes course, so we don't have to wait in line."

"Excellent," Tess answered, pulling the hat down over her face again.

"Hey, they have gourmet cooking classes, taught

by professional chefs. The ones that are still available are Vegan and Malaysian."

"Sweet! Let's take the Malaysian class. I can't believe there are still spots open – they have great food."

Kallie touched the screen a few times and announced that they were signed up. "I thought that'd get your attention. And— now I'm hungry."

"Me too," Tess agreed, swinging her legs off the lounge chair and slipping on her turquoise flip flops. "Let's grab some lunch before the tour. Think they have a Malaysian restaurant?"

"I doubt it. But I know they have Thai."

"Let's go!"

* * * * *

The young, well-dressed tour guide called their small group together at the end of the check-in desk – there were only eight of them – and held up a small yellow sign with a smiley face on it. Kallie suspected she'd be sweating buckets if she wore a suit in this weather, even inside the air-conditioned ship, but he looked cool and happy.

"I carry this sign so you can always find me if we get separated, but I probably won't need it with a group this size. We're going counterclockwise around the ship on this tour, so if you remember that, you shouldn't get lost."

There were no children in the group, so the guide didn't clarify, but Kallie wasn't sure if she knew which way was counterclockwise. Tess pointed down a nearby hallway.

A woman close to them whispered, "At least he didn't start saying 'starboard' and 'aft' – then I'd definitely be lost."

The ship turned out to be almost fifteen years old, they learned. It was maintained in perfect condition and was regularly upgraded with all of the newest gadgets and attractions, the tour guide told them.

"Fifteen years is old enough to produce plenty of ghosts for a tour, apparently," Kallie whispered to Tess, sounding hopeful.

"No way, Kallie. I like sleeping."

"Chicken."

Tess clucked quietly in agreement.

"A bit of interesting trivia," the guide began, standing outside an arched entranceway to the kids' zone. "This bouncy castle room is currently the largest inflatable bounce house on any existing cruise ship in the world – and it's also the single most popular spot for wedding photos on the entire ship."

The whole group laughed, and Kallie pictured a

crowded room full of brides in elegant white gowns jumping happily on the giant inflatable drawbridge.

"We'll break here for a minute so anyone can go get photos if they'd like—" the guide started to add, but they were already off and running.

"Take off your shoes!" he yelled after them.

"Will we be going down to the engine rooms?" Kallie asked the guide when they had all reassembled.

"I'm afraid we don't offer that tour anymore," he answered. "It's a security risk, and it's really not that much fun. The engines are incredibly loud, and we'd all need to wear ear protection."

Kallie nodded, understanding.

"There's a great video about the engines on the cruise channel," an older man in their group told them. "I'm sure it's not as interesting as seeing them up close, but it's very informative. They were manufactured in Finland, and you won't believe how huge they are."

Kallie thanked him, as the group moved on toward the next feature.

"I don't know how we're going to solve this mystery if we can't follow in the exact steps of the victim," Tess mumbled to Kallie, teasingly.

"Oh, fear not. We'll find a way," Kallie replied with a scheming grin.

Walking back to their room after the tour, Tess inspected the tour map and rotated it to match the way they were walking. As they passed the section that would be closest to the engines, she pointed it out.

"This hallway should go back in that direction. Apart from being boring and loud, the tour probably avoids the engines because they would tend to encourage troublemaking decisions – but we can find it ourselves."

"I'm sure we wouldn't be able to get to the actual engines," Kallie mentioned.

"No, they'll be locked up tight. But I'm sure the victim didn't get there either. We can see up through all the balconies from here, so I'll bet this is where Samantha looked down and saw him walking." Tess pointed up, and Kallie realized they could see all the way up to their floor. "I just want to see where he was going. I somehow doubt that it was as innocently nerdy as his wife implied."

"You never know about people and their hobbies," Kallie replied, "but I think you're right. We'll just take a quick look in that hallway and then scoot right back to the pool."

* * * * *

117

"What's that sound?" Kallie asked about fifteen yards down the ugly, utilitarian hallway. She was trying to whisper, but the background noise was already growing loud.

"Shhh!" Tess whispered back.

"It sounds like someone crying. Or singing."

Tess stopped and listened. She put her hand on the cheaply paneled wall and then turned back to Kallie. "It's just the ship's engines, listen. It does sound like it's wailing, because we're so close."

Kallie didn't need to put her ear to the wall – the tour guide was right, it was incredibly loud, and they weren't even very close yet. But when she touched it, she could feel the vibration in her bones. "Weird, it's like a banshee in my grandmother's old stories."

"Ugh, wasn't a banshee a harbinger of death? Let's not go there."

"Good point," Kallie whispered back, as they kept walking. She wasn't sure why they were whispering, since it was noisy enough down here to rattle her teeth, but it seemed like a good idea.

Devin's wife said she'd seen him checking out this hallway, but they weren't sure exactly what they were looking for. Maybe he was just lost or got turned around looking for the elevator. That had happened to Kallie and Tess twice.

Or maybe he was meeting someone back here, Kallie considered. There were no cabins so close to the engines, but there were plenty of storage rooms. Surely there were electronics and facility access panels too, but no one seemed to suspect sabotage.

Since there was no passenger foot traffic down here, it wasn't cleaned as well as the main corridors. It wasn't messy, but looked like it hadn't been vacuumed in a few days. The wall paneling and carpet were ugly and plain. Serviceable but dingy – nothing a paying traveler would ever see.

"He was probably just meeting some sleazy shipboard fling or buying drugs or something." Kallie was starting to get a whopper of a headache from the noise, and she wasn't feeling the greatest faith in humanity at the moment.

"Or maybe he saw something shady and was trying to be a hero?"

Kallie groaned. "Don't say that. I already feel sorry for his poor wife and daughter, let's not make him a dead hero too."

Tess agreed with a crooked smile. "Agreed. Definitely a mad bomber who was stopped by a brave and valiant deck hand."

"Much better."

"Until we find out otherwise."

"Of course," Kallie nodded, as they approached a corner, watching carefully for strangers.

"Ouch," Tess suddenly yelped, bending down to grab her foot.

"What happened?"

"I didn't see this broken glass, and I got a sliver in my toe," Tess explained, with annoyance. Her tiny flip-flops barely protected her feet – which didn't matter at the pool, but there was a smashed wine glass in the hallway. Nearby, a plate lay upside-down on the carpet, tilted against the wall.

Tess leaned against the wall and yanked out the small glass shard, applying pressure to the cut. "I wonder why this glass is even here. Surely the engineers aren't drinking down here."

"Do I need to repeat my slimy tryst theory?"

"This isn't exactly the most romantic spot for a rendezvous," Tess observed.

"True, but it's pretty private."

Tess nodded at that with a repulsed expression. "Hey, what's under that plate?"

"What? Where?" Kallie walked over to the plate and saw something underneath it. Bending down, she could see it was a key card. "It's just someone's room key."

"It doesn't belong to a cruise worker," Tess replied, "They all have their cards on lanyards, like Daphne's."

"You think it belongs to the victim, don't you?"

Kallie asked, intrigued.

"Who else would've been down here?"

"We should call Reilly and let him know we found it," Kallie added. "I wonder why it would've been sitting here for two days?"

"This place is gross. I doubt anyone comes down here. Unless they're looking for a slimy tryst, I mean," Tess added with a grin.

"Do you think he was poisoned right here?" Kallie whispered.

"Ugh, Kallie, don't say that."

"Well, something happened right here. It looks like there was a fight. Maybe—"

Suddenly a rough voice called out, "Who's down here?" and they both jumped in fear.

Crouching down, Tess grabbed the key card and whispered, "Let's get out of here!" as the voice grew closer, now just around the corner of the hallway. And they both ran.

Chapter Eight

Kallie and Tess hurried down the dingy, deserted hallway, as quickly as possible without appearing to be obviously running in fear. Tess tried the handle of the first door in the hallway, but it was locked. The next four were also locked. And the fifth.

"We need to find a place to hide," she whispered, desperation growing in her voice. The constant thrumming noise of the engines masked the distance of their follower.

"Remember the part about us *not* being in danger this time? I *liked* that part." Kallie tried the next door and found it slightly ajar.

They peeked in, to see if it was empty, and saw nothing but shadows. *A good sign? Or a trap?* Kallie glanced back down the hallway.

They were out of time.

"Come on," Kallie whispered, as she slipped through the doorway. When Tess followed, she closed it silently and found that it locked behind them.

The room was dark, but there were slivers of light coming from the covered windows. As they waited and listened, their eyes gradually adjusted to the dim light. The room was huge and almost completely empty. A few chairs were stacked against one wall.

They leaned against the cheap paneling as they both caught their breath.

"Do you think that was really the murderer chasing us?" Kallie asked when her heartbeat had mostly slowed back to normal.

"With our luck? Probably."

"Let's see the key."

"Oh, right." Tess handed over the key card, which was still clutched in her fist. "I wish I'd taken a picture of it first, but I was afraid the killer was coming back to clean up."

"I think you were right," Kallie agreed. She flipped the small, plastic card over, inspecting it closely. "It doesn't have any writing on it." The room keys didn't normally have any markings except the HappySail logo, but many of the passengers decorated them with stickers or markers to personalize them.

"The concierge can scan it to find the owner. And it probably has fingerprints on it."

"Oops." Kallie winced and handed it back carefully, holding it only by the edges. "Good point."

"We can take it to the security office later. Do you think it's safe to go back out yet?"

"That guy was definitely chasing us, whether he

was the killer or just an angry employee," Kallie replied. "So we're going to be in trouble either way. Let's wait a few more minutes, until he's gone, just in case."

They sat in silence while their eyes continued to adjust in the darkened space.

"What is this place, some kind of meeting room?" Kallie asked, looking around.

"I guess so. It's bigger than any of the dining rooms. And all of the big entertainment rooms are on higher floors. So this must be a conference room."

"But why would you have a conference room on a cruise ship? How boring," Kallie laughed.

"After the last legal conference I attended in Chicago with Winchester, I wouldn't mind one with spa treatments and piña coladas," Tess replied, rolling her eyes. "I think we gave that guy the slip," she added, walking back toward the door. "Should we go back to the room?"

"Let's give it a few more minutes, in case he's still looking," Kallie added, feeling less than heroic. "I don't think he got a good look at us, but I'm pretty sure we're the only ones in this hallway. If we open the door, it'll be a dead giveaway."

They walked around the huge, empty conference room, approaching the windows to see if they could get a look outside. The drapes were heavy fabric, more like pool covers than curtains. They pulled back a corner and peered out, but could see only water.

"Wasn't this meant to be a fun trip?" Kallie sighed. "How do we keep stumbling into these crazy situations?"

"Wouldn't we be bored, if we went six months without a madman chasing us around?" Tess answered sarcastically.

"Hopefully we'll find out in the *next* six months," Kallie replied with a chuckle. "Hey, is that an old fax machine? Have we stumbled into a technology graveyard?"

"Where?" Tess asked, looking around the dim room.

"Over in the corner," Kallie answered, walking toward the shadowy equipment.

"I can't really see– Oh, it's a paper shredder."

"Who brings a paper shredder on a cruise ship?"

"It probably belongs to the cruise company," Tess answered, sensibly. "They have a lot of sensitive information, like credit cards and passports and stuff."

"Mmm-hmm," Kallie replied absently. Her curiosity was getting the best of her, and she made her way closer.

"Or maybe there's a paper shredder convention on board. Hosted by lobsters. And... you're not even listening," Tess replied with a sigh. "Don't you *dare* start looking through those papers."

"I'm not looking..." Kallie mumbled, as she

inquisitively picked through the stack of printed pages with one fingernail.

"Yes, you are. You're going to get us arrested for identity theft," Tess hissed.

"It's not passports and stuff," Kallie added quietly. "I think they're copies of letters."

"Letters?" Tess asked, grudgingly creeping up for a look.

"Typed letters, not handwritten."

"Business stuff?" Tess asked, leaning around Kallie's shoulder with new interest.

"No, it seems personal, even though it's all neatly typed."

"Why shred them, then?" Tess wondered aloud.

"Maybe bad memories, of an old flame?" Kallie suggested with a shrug.

"Maybe evidence tying someone to a *murder*?"

"Maybe we're being *paranoid*?" Kallie replied with a smirk. But she leaned closer to the stack, trying to read the top sheet in the dim light.

"Some of the pages are already shredded," Tess noted, looking at the tiny scraps of paper in the ejection bin. "The person must've been stopped before they could finish. Maybe it jammed. Or someone surprised them."

"This one is just an ordinary letter. No gooey love notes, no threats, no nothing."

"Well, go on to the next page then," her best friend replied with a laugh. "We're already in this up to our necks."

Kallie flipped to the next page. "Boring. Same thing."

"Why would anyone shred this?" Tess asked, shaking her head in confusion. "Can you even tell who they were sent to?"

"No. There's no..." Kallie paused.

"Salutation?"

"Lordy, Tess," Kallie laughed quietly. "Yeah, there's no *salutation* at the top. They must've already shredded that page."

"Well, keep going. There must be something bad in here, even if it's just proof of acquaintance."

"Proof of acquaintance," Kallie repeated with a laugh. "Salutation. I'm glad *you* work for the lawyer, and not me." She scanned down the next page and a moment later, she added, "Whoa. This page says, 'my wife died in August, because we could no longer afford the chemotherapy treatments.'"

"What?!"

"Look," Kallie replied, pointing at the page so Tess could read around her shoulder. "It says 'When he destroyed our company, we lost our small business medical insurance."

"Oh no. Is this some kind of *manifesto*?" Tess

whispered, horrified.

"No, I think it's..." Kallie flipped to the next page. "It says 'I'm only requesting that you review the case, your honor.' I think this is a letter to a *judge*."

"You know what—?" Tess started, then paused. She suddenly grabbed the whole stack of papers and shoved them into her pool bag. "If we leave them, they'll just get shredded. We'll take these to Officer Reilly in the security office, too."

"Good idea, now let's get out of here. I feel like a sitting duck."

Stopping only to listen at the door for a moment, they snuck back out the way they came, still feeling like they were being watched by a thousand eyes.

* * * * *

After running back to their suite to quickly change clothes, Kallie and Tess only had a few minutes before their reservation on the ship's very popular ropes course. They both put on tennis shoes and hurried back out to the elevator.

Kallie had been dreading the treacherous experience, high above the Lido deck, but it turned out to be easier than she expected. Tess was always a superstar at this kind of activity, but the safety harness made Kallie braver than her usual nature.

"Look, Tess! I'm a monkey," she called, climbing her pegged wooden pole at high speed, as the wind howled around them.

"You've always been a monkey," Tess shouted back from her own pole, laughing out loud.

Kallie ran across the thick metal wire, clasping the support line above her, "This is so much fun! We need to do this at home!"

"You bet, Kal! I know a perfect place in Clearwater," Tess stared after Kallie, obviously surprised and delighted at her best friend's sudden adventurousness.

They both ran and jumped and swung across the sky, and then finally slid down a zip line back to the ship's deck below.

"Let's do it again!" Kallie said with a laugh.

Tess pointed back at the long line of people waiting. "Let's try to book another time from the pool. But I doubt there are any more spots open today."

They started walking back to the pool, and Tess just had to add, "I'm so proud of you, Kal. I thought you'd hate it."

"I did too," Kallie laughed self-consciously. "I hope we can go again."

* * * * *

Tess was lounging on their suite's oversized couch with a book, after an afternoon of clandestine snooping – followed by acrobatics and lazily relaxing poolside, while Kallie repainted her toenails on the balcony before dinner. When she returned back inside with a fresh baby blue pedicure, Kallie walked over to the dresser. A moment later, she frowned and then flipped over the room service menu and cruise magazine.

"Hey, Tess. I can't find that key card we found. Do you know where it is?"

"The one we found downstairs?" Tess looked up from her book. "I thought you were going to give it to the security guys."

"I was, and Officer Reilly told us to meet him at six o'clock, so I set the key *right* here where I wouldn't forget to take it to him. I'm sure we're overreacting and it's probably completely unrelated to the murder, but I *swear*, it was right here on the dresser, next to the tv."

"Maybe it got knocked behind the furniture." Tess tried peeking behind the dresser, but it was too dark to see anything. "At least my poor phone will finally get some use, out here in the signal-free zone," she sighed, taking it out of her purse. She turned on the screen flashlight, then used it to look behind the dresser.

"Anything?"

Tess made a revolted face. "It's too gross for

words. But no key."

"Where else could it have gone?" Kallie asked, checking the drawers. "Housekeeping wouldn't have taken an unmarked key."

"You don't think someone else took it, do you?"

Kallie started to say no, of course not – but then crumpled onto the couch with a sigh, remembering the dead man on the buffet table. "I don't know. I mean, who would break into our room to steal a stupid plastic key card?"

"A killer?" Tess responded with a crooked smile.

Kallie smirked and rolled her eyes. "There's no way we just *happened* to find the–"

"Really?" Tess interrupted with a raised eyebrow. "I mean, it wouldn't be the first time."

"Don't remind me!" Kallie groaned theatrically.

"Okay, well, it's gone," Tess concluded, after joining the search. "Maybe we can ask the housekeeper if she saw anyone come out of our room. If someone let themselves in, then they must either have a master key – or they snuck past her."

"Or bribed her. Or stole her master key too."

"Well, we'll see what she says," Tess replied with a shrug. "There are cameras in the hallway, so if she didn't see anything, we can ask security to check the cameras."

"Officer, come quick! Someone stole our super-important, unmarked, probably irrelevant key card!" Kallie squeaked.

Tess snorted back a laugh. "We're not going to even *mention* the key. You already put yourself in danger once, solving the murder in Owhiro. We're keeping a low profile on this one. No one can protect us out here if we antagonize a killer. We'll just say it was jewelry or something."

* * * * *

Sitting in Reilly's office for their planned meeting a short time later, they all leaned close to a computer screen. On the video, the dark-clothed intruder ran from the room, crashing into the housekeeping cart outside the door and knocking over the pile of towels stacked on top. A moment later, the stack of paper-wrapped soaps and tiny shampoo bottles also tipped over.

Reilly paused the remarkably clear footage and leaned even closer.

"Can you see his face?" Kallie asked.

"No, he's facing the wrong way," the security officer sighed. "I think he's purposely avoiding the cameras."

As he restarted the video, the housekeeper came into view, from the next room. She stood over the mess of linens and toiletries on the floor, looking dismayed. It was clear that she hadn't seen what happened. Luckily, none of the shampoo bottles had broken, but they had flown and rolled a ridiculous distance in the hallway.

"That's all, just those fifteen seconds," Reilly told them. "An unusually brazen act, and we'll step up security. And we'll keep analyzing the video, obviously. I'll let you know if we find out anything else."

"Thank you so much for checking. And for taking us seriously," Kallie sighed. "We were just going to ask the housekeeper if she'd seen anything."

"It's no trouble, Miss Brooks. It's all easily accessible on the computer," he patted the oversized monitor on his desk like it was a golden retriever. "Are you sure you don't want to file an official complaint?"

"No, thank you. The bracelet that he stole wasn't expensive, it was just a knock-off," Kallie fibbed cautiously. "Thanks again."

* * * * *

Once they were alone in their suite again, Kallie asked, "What are we doing, attracting a murderer into our own room? Are we crazy?"

"Yep," Tess answered, hugging her.

"That must be the person who stole the key,

right?" It seemed crazy that they had been joking about it just a few hours before, now that they'd seen video footage of some creepy thief right in their own room. "But how did he know where to look?"

"Someone must've seen us pick up the key in that hallway," Tess answered. "But there was no way of knowing it would end up like this. *We're* not the crazy ones here, Kal."

Kallie was pulling the last few shampoo bottles out from under the bed where they had rolled off of the housekeeping cart.

Tess added, "Well, we're meeting with that federal agent tomorrow morning for our interview. It's too bad we can't give them the key, but we can tell him what happened. Then we'll be safely out of it, and we can go back to relaxing without looking over our shoulders."

"Do you think we're in danger, Tess?" Kallie asked, wincing.

"Probably," Tess replied with a serious nod, and then shrugged. "But the robber won't do anything to us with other people around, and the FBI on board. So let's get ready for dinner, and we'll figure out the next steps from there."

"That makes sense – safety in numbers. Nothing disinfects better than sunlight, as my dad likes to say. What are you wearing?" Kallie asked, trying to shake off her nerves. "It's the big Captain's Dinner, and I heard they always have a photographer. We must dress to the nines, my *dahling*."

"We should definitely wear our best dresses," Tess answered. "My yellow one and your green one. This will be the perfect night to wear them, and the message board did say there would be a *professional* photographer–"

Kallie ran to the mirror and sighed. "I'll definitely need to fix my hair, then. It's all frizzy from the salty air."

* * * * *

The photographer obviously had a crush on Tess – he took several pictures of her and Kallie, as he made his rounds of the dining room. But then he came around to their table a second time, and then a third.

"At least we'll get a wide choice of pictures," Tess shrugged.

"I hope I'm in them," Kallie winced, as the goofy photographer made another painfully awkward pass at Tess. "Do you think he's cropping me out of them?"

"Probably," Tess sighed. "What a weirdo. Let's get up and move around, then he'll have to get both of us – we'll keep him on his toes."

"And I'll have evidence of this cute dress. I'll probably never wear it again, and I want pictures."

They finished the last bites of their meals quickly, then stood up and walked aimlessly around the room, as the photographer followed them like a puppy. Occasionally they'd turn and pose together, to his delight. If he got too close, they'd switch sides and keep moving.

"This feels like the world's slowest game of 'freeze tag,' but I thought everyone outgrew that in second grade."

Tess laughed, but repeated "Weirdo," under her breath.

* * * * *

After the photographer moved on to other passengers in the restaurant, Kallie and Tess sat back down at their table and were quickly approached by another couple.

"Do you mind if we join you?" the woman asked. "We usually sit with another group, but they don't like attending the formal dress events. It seems strange to sit alone on a cruise, somehow."

"Of course!" Kallie answered, pushing out the other chairs with her foot.

"So you two have been on a cruise before?" Tess asked the friendly older woman.

"We try to go every year, since we're both retired

now. You can get a great price if you're flexible on your dates."

"Luckily, we're flexible *and* cheap," her husband added with a laugh.

"We actually met on a cruise in Alaska. I was there with my daughter, and he was the best man in a wedding party."

"Tess says we should avoid meeting guys on the ship," Kallie quipped.

"Absolutely!" she replied. "Look at the trouble you might end up with!" She nudged her husband in the ribs, and he gave her a big, noisy kiss on the cheek.

Tess and Kallie both laughed.

"We've been so lucky about getting seated with cool people," Kallie told them. "I was worried when they told us about this mixed table concept."

"Oh, believe me – we've had some doozies!" She turned to her husband. "Remember the couple who were trying to get abducted by aliens?"

"They kept going up to the top deck and waving a flashlight, insisting that 'this was the place.'"

"And we weren't even in the Bermuda Triangle, or anything," she added, shaking her head. "I've never seen anyone so disappointed, when we all got back to Miami safely."

"As long as they don't try to discuss politics," her husband added. "Or talk about their work through the entire dinner, or show us ten thousand baby pictures, I'm fine with just about anyone."

"I don't mind the baby pictures," his wife amended.

"I'd rather see dog pictures," he answered with a grin.

Kallie laughed. "Oh, if you want dog pictures, I've got you covered."

"Let's see them! We have three dogs at home; they're staying with my daughter," his wife held up her phone and swapped with Kallie, admiring the photos of Sherman.

"Hey, did you just see that?" Kallie asked quietly, nudging Tess.

"What?"

"That guy just stuck a knife in his pocket." Kallie nodded toward a couple sitting three tables away, not wanting to point.

"A knife from the table? Are you sure?" Tess asked, doubtfully.

"Uh, pretty sure."

"That's encouraging," Tess replied with a crooked smirk.

"I mean, he picked up the knife and stuck it under the tablecloth, and never put it back." The room was unusually noisy, with loud discussions about everyone's formal clothing and the elegant dishes on the menu – and the roving photographer added to the commotion. Obviously no one could hear their quiet conversation, but Kallie found herself whispering anyway.

"Maybe he dropped it," Tess shrugged.

"And *that's* why I'm not screaming yet…" Kallie agreed, hesitantly.

Tess was being her normal stoic self, but they both remembered that there was a murderer on board.

Kallie looked around, but there were no security guards in the dining room. The other couple at their table was chatting together quietly, and she didn't want to alarm them needlessly.

"Okay, hang on. I'm just going to check." Kallie stood up, stumbling a little in her heels, not entirely sure if she was pretending to be tipsy – when anyone could see she was drinking iced tea – or if it was just nerves.

She walked toward the suspicious party's table and clumsily dropped her purse. Sighing in annoyance, she squatted down to pick it up, kneeling and stretching to grab a lipstick which had fortuitously rolled close to the man's chair. Having collected her belongings, she stood up and returned to her own table.

"The knife isn't under the table," she whispered to Tess.

"That was actually pretty subtle. For you." Tess was teasing her, but she actually looked a little impressed.

"Thanks, I think," Kallie replied, brushing the carpet lint off her new purse. "So now what do we do about the knife?"

"There could be a perfectly rational explanation, you know," Tess replied.

"One that doesn't end in another dead body? Tell me." Kallie raised an eyebrow and waited expectantly.

"I haven't figured it out yet, either. We should probably just tell a waiter or something."

"And stay out of it?" Kallie asked, incredulously.

"Doesn't that sound like a *great* idea? For a change?"

"It does, but I think we both know it's not going to happen."

Tess tilted her head and shrugged, noncommittally.

"They're almost finished with their dinner," Kallie whispered, pushing back her plate as if she had just finished eating. "Let's follow them."

"Seriously?"

"At least far enough to see if he's walking funny. We'll be able to tell if he has that big knife jabbing him in the thigh."

"And if he does?" Tess asked.

"We'll burn that bridge when we get to it. Come on."

"I have a better idea," Tess insisted. "I'll go find a waiter to help us. You just keep an eye on him until I get back."

"Okay, but hurry. They're already eating dessert, so they probably won't be much longer."

Tess left to find backup support, while Kallie tried to watch the other table without being too obvious. She still didn't see the missing knife.

Should I walk past them again? Maybe the knife is on the table and I just can't see it from here.

Before she decided, though, the couple stood up and placed their napkins on the table, apparently ready to leave. Kallie watched them, trying to determine if the man was walking strangely.

Oh man, he's definitely limping. But is it knife-down-the-pants limping or sitting-too-long-and-my-foot's-asleep limping?

"I just hope it's not prosthetic-leg limping," she mumbled to herself nervously as she stood up, still deciding how to intercept them. "This evening has been awkward enough."

Tess, where are you? Hurry up.

Luckily, the question of how to stop them answered itself, as she turned to look for Tess and clumsily stumbled right into the woman, knocking her against the table.

"Oh my goodness, I'm so sorry!" Kallie gasped, completely in earnest. She'd thought the couple was going in the other direction, toward the doors.

"No, it's my fault," the woman replied, wiping iced tea off her skirt. "We were leaving, but I wanted to take one last look at the island out of these windows, before it gets too dark. I heard we're finally setting sail again tomorrow." She gestured toward the huge picture window at the rear of the restaurant, where evening was settling over Cozumel. "My husband and I were married here, fifteen years ago."

"Oh, I'm sorry about that too," Kallie sighed miserably. This whole knife-attacker interception wasn't going exactly as she'd planned.

She glanced over the woman's shoulder and saw Tess talking to a waiter. She was pointing in Kallie's direction, and the rather large waiter was watching the three of them closely.

"I'll walk over there with you," Kallie added to the now-rumpled woman, smiling cheerfully. "Maybe you can point out where you were married. It's a pretty small island, right?"

She and the woman walked toward the expansive window, which was tinted to avoid the daytime glare but still showed the island in gorgeous evening color. The lights at the port were coming on, increasing the charm.

"You can probably see it from here. We got married on the beach and there was a little wooden gazebo. It was so romantic—"

Kallie could hear the woman's husband clomping loudly behind them and hoped the waiter was watching.

"Oh, this is really beautiful," Kallie replied with a sigh, gazing at the white sand beaches in the failing light and absently hoping the crime would be solved quickly and they'd finally get to visit the island the next day.

"We've been through a lot in the past two years, and we were going to renew our—"

"Excuse me, sir," a man's voice spoke behind them. "I need to see what you're carrying."

They both turned around from the window and saw the waiter addressing the husband. He wasn't touching the man, but his expression and demeanor showed it wasn't a request. Kallie wondered if the cruise waitstaff had to take security training, like flight attendants.

"I don't know what you're talking about," the man squeaked anxiously. He opened his empty hands, displaying his palms. "I'm not carrying anything."

"In your trousers, sir. I can see that you've taken something. It's affecting your walk."

The man sighed, turned a painful shade of scarlet and awkwardly, slowly pulled a huge bread knife out of his pants.

The waiter grabbed the man's wrist and yanked the knife away, facing no resistance.

"We heard there was a murderer on board," he whined. "I was just trying to protect my wife."

"It's a bread knife," Kallie noted quietly. "You couldn't even poke someone with it."

His wife was completely enamored by the gesture, though. "Oh, Charles. You wanted to protect me? That's the nicest thing you've said to me in years," she cooed happily, rushing forward to throw her arms around his neck and kiss him.

"Okay, you're both coming to security with me," the waiter grumbled, separating them. "Thank you, miss," he added to Tess.

Tess waved at him as she crossed to Kallie's side by the window. "So we didn't catch a killer, but we did our good deed for the day, I think. He probably would've just hurt himself with that thing."

"Almost definitely," Kallie answered with a nod. "Come look at this view of the island."

Chapter Nine

After sleepily carrying their coffee to the pool the next morning, and drinking it in the peaceful, breezy shade, Kallie was unexpectedly nudged by Tess. The captain and the federal agent had joined Reilly back on the deck, where they were watching the pilot tend to the helicopter.

The three men were speaking too quietly for the girls to hear them, but they apparently came to a conclusion – and Kallie saw the captain nod in approval and return to his duties. Reilly and the agent followed him a few minutes later, still talking.

"We really should go tell that agent everything we know," Kallie sighed. "Even if we don't have the actual key anymore, we can tell him what we saw and heard. He'll understand that it's a possible clue. And even if it turns out to be nothing, we did our duty – and it's officially his case now, anyway."

"Look at you, being all responsible," Tess replied with a wink. "You're right, let's go tell him. They're probably going back to Reilly's office."

They stood up and collected their belongings – in case the agent needed to speak to them further, after they told him about the key and the broken wine glass. But when they entered the double doors, they found the agent alone in the hallway inside. Reilly must've already returned to his office.

"Excuse me, sir?" Kallie called out, politely. "We wanted to tell–"

The federal agent they'd seen on deck glanced toward them, briefly made eye contact with Kallie, and abruptly turned and walked away.

Seriously?

"Excuse me? Sir?" Kallie repeated, louder, but she watched in surprise as the agent disappeared down the hallway.

"Wow, that was rude," Tess sneered.

"I mean, he heard me, right?" Kallie asked.

"Obviously."

That's our cavalry? The hero who was supposed to save the day?

"What a jerk," Kallie complained. "I mean, we're trying to help with his investigation. We have an actual clue."

"Well, *had*," Tess replied with a slight smile.

"True, but that's hardly the point. He's going to spend hours, if not days, questioning hundreds of people who know nothing about the murder. And he just pointedly ignored the only two people on board who know anything."

"Apart from the murderer," Tess added.

"The murderer's *probably* not talking." Kallie reflected for a minute. "Well, I'm sure he'll be fine. That's why he's a federal agent and we're just two sunbathing vacationers frolicking at sea. He doesn't need our help. We'll just leave him to his hundreds of pointless, boring interviews while we sip another perfect key lime smoothie by the pool."

"And can we go back to our leisurely stakeout now, Miss Poirot?" Tess asked with a slightly sinister grin. "Since the *gendarmes* are here to protect us?"

"*Mais, oui.* Might as well." Kallie answered with a wink.

Now that someone else is protecting Skylar and Samantha – and us – we can go back to our whodunnit game with no worries.

"Now let's go get this interview over with," Tess sighed, drinking the last of her coffee. "Maybe we'll get five minutes in Cozumel before the ship has to leave."

Their group was being interviewed in the main dining room, but they had plenty of time before the nine o'clock appointment, and they grudgingly arrived a little early.

An hour later, though, they were still sitting by the window of the restaurant, waiting impatiently, like everyone else, for the official interviews to start. In the meantime, Kallie was trying to get a Wi-Fi signal from the dock at Cozumel.

"Come on, you stupid phone." She tipped and tilted it every possible way, pressed it against the glass and thrust it over her head.

"No luck?" Tess asked.

"No," Kallie sighed. "We can practically touch the Cozumel dock from here. Why can't I get their signal?"

"Emergency at home?" Missy asked, sitting down next to them.

"Oh, hi Missy! No emergency, she just wants to video chat with her dog."

Instead of laughing, Missy nodded in understanding. "I hear you, girl. I brought about fifty video clips of my two terriers, when I heard how expensive it is to use your phone at sea."

"And even with the ship's onboard Wi-Fi, you can't do video conferencing unless you pay for the most expensive package," Tess agreed.

Kallie stood up and jokingly raised her phone in one hand and a fork in the other, like an old-fashioned tv-top antenna. She stuck out one foot and suddenly cheered quietly, "Oh my gosh, it worked!" But as soon as she pulled the phone close enough to see the screen, the signal was lost again.

She sat back down with a thump, and a disappointed expression swept over her face.

"You'll just have to wait until we get out there,

Kal," Tess consoled her. They said it'll only be a few more hours."

* * * * *

Once the full list of interviewees for the morning session had been checked off, the assisting security officer closed the main double doors to the restaurant, essentially locking them all in. The small but strangely intimidating interview table was set up near another door, where Kallie presumed they would eventually exit.

The federal agent stood up and introduced himself, explaining briefly why he was there.

"Ladies and gentlemen," he began, drawing their attention and silencing the chatter. "My name is Agent Christopher Paul, with the FBI. I know many of you haven't yet been informed, but there has been a death on the ship, and—"

He waited again for the sudden flurry of whispers to quiet down.

"I'm here to investigate. I'll make these interviews as quick as possible, but we do need to speak with everyone."

"Why weren't we told about this before?" a shocked-sounding woman asked loudly.

"Who died? Was it a murder?" someone else

asked.

A man in the back of the room snapped, "Obviously it was a murder, or the FBI wouldn't be here."

"I heard it was that shady lawyer with all the billboards by Disneyworld," an older man added, and a few other voices agreed with him.

To Kallie's horror, another man answered, "Good riddance," and a few others agreed with his opinion too. She looked toward the corner and saw the widow crying openly at a small table. Her friend Helen held Skylar in her arms, and the formerly brave pre-teen was sobbing despondently.

No one else seemed to notice them, and Kallie was on the verge of saying something herself, when Officer Navarro stood up and snapped angrily, "The family of the victim is in the room! Please *hold* your nasty opinions."

Several jaws audibly snapped shut in embarrassment, or at least an ounce of decorum.

The female officer shot a look at Agent Paul, that telegraphed a heartfelt longing to punch him, but he continued his introduction, oblivious.

"We're proceeding with these interviews in sections, by floor of the ship, so I'll be calling you in room order, not alphabetically. Please approach the interview table quickly when your name is called, and we'll all try to get out of here post-haste."

He sat down at the table and Officer Navarro called the first name.

* * * * *

The interviews went slower than expected, and Tess and Kallie soon gave up their hope for a quick exit. Instead, they distractedly foraged for breakfast at the busy buffet and then returned to their table to eat. Kallie watched over her best friend's shoulder – discreetly, she hoped – as she stuck a forkful of scrambled eggs in her mouth.

"Are you eating eggs? What's wrong with you?" Tess asked with a worried scowl.

"Shhh," Kallie whispered, then looked at her fork briefly before putting it down with a surprised look of disgust.

"You hate eggs."

Grabbing her friend's glass of tomato juice and guzzling half of it to wash the horrid taste of the eggs out of her mouth, she whispered, "That FBI guy is talking to the victim's wife, Tess. Let me listen."

"Ohhh." Tess quickly switched seats so she could see them too.

The new widow leaned against the table, obviously still grief-stricken, talking to the federal agent without making eye contact. Her daughter, who had previously wanted to seem so cool and detached, was still leaning on Helen's shoulder at the corner table. The agent didn't seem appropriately sympathetic to Kallie, but perhaps he hadn't heard their alibi yet.

He must have spoken to Reilly about her, so how can he still consider her a suspect?

"I can't hear them," Tess whispered.

"Neither can I. But it looks like that jerk is being just as rude to her as he was to me."

"What a shock," Tess grumbled.

"I'm surprised he'd talk to her in the dining room. Shouldn't that be a private conversation?"

"Maybe he talked to her privately with Officer Reilly first," Tess suggested. "After the ship's captain, she must've been the most important person on his list."

"So this is just a follow-up, in case he had any more questions?" Kallie shrugged. "Samantha did tell Helen that she was going to wait and tell the FBI about seeing her husband in that hallway, since she didn't consider the security team to be 'real' police. Maybe she's giving him the details about that. And her husband's affair."

"It doesn't look like he's listening to her, though," Tess observed. "He's the one doing all the talking. I hate the way he's leaning over the table at her, like he's accusing her of something. I think she's still crying."

"She has an alibi, for heaven's sake," Kallie agreed with a sneer. "Now he's just harassing her. In public. I like this guy less and less all the time."

"Me too. Maybe he thinks she witnessed something that she hasn't mentioned yet. If she did, he needs to know that too," Tess answered. "Speaking of which – have you seen those women that were outside the restaurant the next morning?"

"Jannie and her friends, you mean? The murder experts?" Kallie asked with a laugh. Then she glanced around the dining room with concern. "You know, I actually haven't seen them at all."

They both looked around for the gossipers, and Tess asked, "Shouldn't they be in here with us?"

"Maybe they were staying in a different section of the ship. We can ask Reilly about them when we get out of here. Right now, I'm going to get something different from the buffet," Kallie answered, looking down in disgust at her plate.

"I can't believe you got scrambled eggs."

* * * * *

When Skylar's name was called, she walked to the interview table alone, looking scared and even younger than her years. Kallie was glad to see an older woman in a stylish suit immediately approach the table to join her. She sat down next to Skylar and spoke to her quietly, and the girl visibly relaxed. Kallie guessed she was some kind of child advocate, and was relieved that the cruise line had her on board.

With so many kids on the voyage, her services must be needed often – if not usually for murder.

Skylar wasn't at the table for long. Kallie and Tess knew she'd been with her mother getting ice cream when the murder happened, so she couldn't have much else to tell the agent about the events of that night. They saw her nod and shake her head a few times, yes and no, but she didn't seem to be speaking much either.

Agent Paul's manner with the young girl was barely more pleasant than they'd seen with her mother. He leaned forward toward her again and said something with an ugly expression on his face.

They couldn't hear him, but the advocate wasn't having an ounce of it. She stood up fast enough to knock over her chair, and grabbed Skylar's hand in her own. Looking like she wanted to slap the agent, she contented herself with a loud threat, the first comment from the table that they could hear clearly. "If I can't get you *fired*, I'll most definitely see that this is the last time you *ever* interview a child."

Kallie was glad to see her put a comforting arm around the girl and walk her away, ignoring the agent's insistence that his interview wasn't finished.

"Looks like it is, buddy," Kallie sneered quietly.

"Weren't we supposed to get at least one whole day to do nothing?" Tess groaned, after another hour of waiting to be called. "Like, just sit on a lounge chair, read a cheesy novel about vampires in love, and listen to vapid '90s pop songs?"

"I'm pretty sure that was in the contract," Kallie agreed.

"No death, no fights, only minor salacious gossip?" Tess continued. "I don't even care whether it's on a beach or next to a pool. There was supposed to be some 'nothing' involved in this trip."

"At least one day of flipping the off switch in our brains," Kallie agreed. "Possibly with nachos and a strawberry margarita."

"And instead, we've been subjected to murder, mayhem, intruders, and hours of waiting to be interviewed by a mean-spirited, completely unprofessional federal agent."

"And fish trivia."

"Worst of all!" Tess agreed.

"None of this was in the agreement. Even my semi-annual massage and afternoon tea were cancelled for this stupid waiting game."

"Murder and mayhem are becoming our

standard weekend activity, anyway," Tess observed. "And this time your cute boyfriend isn't here to distract us."

"Detective Morrison isn't my boyfriend."

"Mmm-hmm," Tess replied with a grin.

"I do wish he was here, though. He would've had this whole mess straightened out in a heartbeat, and we'd be shopping in Montego Bay right now, instead of waiting on a rude, grumpy, bully of a federal agent who likes picking on a little girl who just lost her dad."

"Morrison would have that murderer crying in his Darjeeling tea and crumpets, confessing to the whole affair," Tess concluded. "And maybe straighten out that fed, too."

"I wouldn't be a bit surprised," Kallie agreed.

Chapter Ten

Kallie watched the late morning rain roll down the windows of the ship as Tess finally got her turn to speak with the federal agent. They had been waiting for almost three hours, as interviewees were called forward and then made their statements and were released. In the meantime, the Mexican coastline had gone from sun-drenched to soggy.

As she watched, the agent's assistant handed over about the hundredth sterile plastic swab in a cellophane wrapper. Tess opened it and swabbed the inside of her cheek, like dozens of people had done before her, and handed it back.

No fingerprinting, Kallie noticed. *So they must have DNA but nothing else*, she thought to herself – *the killer must've worn gloves.* She sighed uncomfortably at all she'd learned about crime since the murder at The Lazy Gecko. It made her feel jaded, and she suddenly wished her friend Detective Morrison really was here, if only to lighten her spirits.

He makes murder interesting, she thought with a sarcastic smirk.

Tess also mostly nodded and shook her head,

not speaking much, Kallie noticed – so they must be routine yes or no questions.

That didn't give Kallie much hope that the agent would solve the murder quickly. As much as she wanted to see the killer caught, get this whole thing resolved, and give Samantha and Skylar the chance to go home where they could grieve in peace – she also wanted to see Cozumel.

This is our first vacation in years, after all! Reilly sounded like the FBI would crack the case in a flash, and we'd be free to go. We didn't ask for this disaster to fall into our laps.

She wanted to video chat with Sherman and go snorkeling and buy a t-shirt, at least. And eat! Besides, Marcy would kill her if she came back without a bottle of local tequila.

Why isn't he asking better questions?

The assisting officer slid a piece of paper across to Tess and she signed it, which was the official end of every interview. She stood up and was escorted to the door of the restaurant, where she turned back to wave at Kallie.

Don't you dare get nervous, Kalliope. You always look guilty when you get nervous.

She took a sip of her now-watery diet coke – trying to ignore the butterflies in her stomach – and braced for her name to be called.

"Kalliope Brooks?" Officer Navarro called.

Standing up, she took a deep breath and approached the small table. The agent acknowledged her and flipped the page in his notebook, asking for her identification, which the officer took from her.

"You're in suite 528, Miss Brooks?" the agent began.

"Yes," she replied quietly, showing her room key even though it wasn't labeled.

"Can you tell me what you saw on the first night of the voyage?"

"We had dinner with some girls we met by the pool," Kallie began, "but we were really late—"

"This was the first night. You'd already made friends with strangers on the first night?" the federal agent asked, suspiciously, sounding as if he'd caught her in a lie.

"Uh, sure," Kallie replied, unclear on why he was asking. "That's the idea, right? Socializing? They're nice girls and we got along well, so we went to dinner."

Something tells me this guy doesn't make friends easily. Especially if he treats everyone like he treated us. And Samantha Devin. And poor Skylar.

"What are their names?"

"Oh, I didn't mean to get them in trouble," Kallie replied. "They were with us the whole evening, not running off to kill anyone."

The agent just blinked at her, waiting.

"I don't even know their last names. Missy and Laura." Kallie didn't point out the sisters at the nearby table, knowing they'd both be called to the interview soon enough.

The agent glanced haughtily at Navarro, who wrote down their names.

Kallie recalled Reilly's statement that the onboard security staff were all retired police officers, and she felt even more annoyed that this former cop was being treated like a 1950s-era secretary. She wondered if he ordered her to get his coffee, too.

Jerk.

"So we were dining late," she continued. "And then after we ate, we were laughing and talking in the restaurant, and suddenly it was almost midnight."

The agent nodded grumpily.

"We thought about calling it a night, but then decided to go to one of the dance clubs instead." Kallie chuckled, then added, "I was wearing these retro boots and Tess said—"

The agent's stony stare convinced her to skip ahead.

"Anyway, it wasn't that crowded in the club, probably because it was the first night and so many people had to fly into Tampa super early to make the departure time." Kallie caught herself again and cut to the chase. "The crowd started to disappear from the dance floor, which seemed weird, and we saw that they were all outside the other door. The door into the hallway."

Finally, the agent seemed to be paying attention.

"We walked out into the hallway, because the bartender mentioned there might be celebrities or a contest, but everyone was just staring down the hall," Kallie described the scene. "We couldn't see anything at first, until people started to get bored and go back to the club. Then we could see the guy on the table."

"The victim?"

"Yeah," Kallie answered. *Who else would be on the table?* "People were laughing because they thought he was drunk from all the free drinks."

"Did *you* think he was drunk?"

"No," she answered simply.

"Did you see anyone acting strangely?"

"No, everyone seemed a little uncomfortable, like the first day of summer camp – when you don't know anyone yet and you don't know where to go," Kallie explained. "But no one seemed suspicious or creepy, just uneasy."

"Was he in the club?" the agent asked.

"What?" Kallie answered, looking at him strangely, "Who? The dead guy? No, he was in the restaurant."

What kind of crazy question is that? Is he

trying to trick me? Or make me tell a lie? Ugh, I hate this guy.

"There's been some suggestion that he might've been in the club earlier."

"Oh. Well, *we* weren't in the club earlier. We got there around midnight."

Definitely trying to catch me in a lie. Oh man, does he think I'm the killer?

Remember how you were going to not get nervous, Kallie? Take a deep breath.

"Then the ship's security team came and chased us all away," she concluded after a brief pause. "That's pretty much the whole story."

"No one seemed overly interested in the victim?"

"*Everyone* was interested. It was so weird how he was all sprawled out on the buffet table like some kind of creepy renaissance painting." She hadn't really thought about the way he'd been draped wildly across the table, and it seemed even stranger in hindsight. *Wouldn't you just collapse?*

The agent nodded once more and then quickly gave her the plastic swab for her DNA sample and asked her to sign the release document.

"You can go. If we have any more questions, we'll contact you."

He turned away as if she'd suddenly become

invisible, and Kallie was reminded again of how much she disliked him. *Rude.* Officer Navarro thanked her, at least, and she left the table.

* * * * *

Reilly caught up to Kallie as she was being escorted from the room, just to tell her that he'd tracked down the hostile wrong number caller.

"I was able to back-trace the extension, and Carol and I stopped by her room and told her to stop harassing other passengers. The woman was really embarrassed, as we expected, and said she was mad at her husband, not you." He added, "And she'd been drinking heavily, obviously."

"Obviously," Kallie agreed with a smile. "Thank you for doing that."

The sudden sound of stomping feet surprised them, and they both turned back toward the interview table.

"Officer Reilly," the federal agent snarled, as he made a beeline for them. "You cannot socialize with possible suspects in this murder. You're undermining both the case and my personal reputation."

Personal reputation? Who in this room full of bored passengers could possibly care about his reputation? Kallie wondered to herself. *Is this guy paranoid, too? Wonderful.*

"We weren't socializing—" Reilly began, before he was cut off.

"I saw you talking, as soon as she stood up."

"He was following up on a different issue," Kallie interjected, annoyed but hoping she could help defuse the situation. "I received a—"

"Both of you, split up. And Officer Reilly, I'll be discussing this with your superiors at the cruise line." The agent spun on his heel and returned to the interview table in a huff.

Reilly watched him go and shook his head.

"Is he always this friendly?" Kallie asked, as they left the restaurant and turned into the hallway.

"Yes," Reilly replied, tersely.

"We tried to give him some potentially helpful information, and he completely ignored us."

"He treats everyone like an infant," Reilly agreed. "Never mind the fact that I have ten times more experience dealing with actual murders in Chicago," he grumbled to himself.

"Oh, so he's new on the job?"

"Straight outta Quantico, as they say," the older officer chuckled sarcastically. "This is his first solo investigation. He thought it would be a simple grab-and-go with the victim's closest relative. It doesn't seem to be his week."

"Grab and go?"

"This is a very unusual case, Miss Brooks. Deaths at sea are tragically not uncommon, but they're almost always due to natural causes or accidents. Or the occasional suicide," he added with a sigh. "Murders are much rarer. But I've personally *never* seen a shipboard murder where the killer wasn't a family member or travel partner. Usually the spouse."

"Oh, so he expected to just grab the wife and jump back on the helicopter?" Kallie asked.

"He's rude, inexperienced, and probably feeling more than a little overwhelmed – but he's not a fool," Reilly conceded. "It's almost *always* a grab-and-go in this situation."

"And they're trusting him with all of these interviews? And the evidence? And all of those DNA samples?"

"Oh, my other officers are capable of keeping that safe," Reilly reassured her. "And he had the sense to bring in some senior officers from the mainland on the copter. Detective Juarez is an old friend, and he's watching that newbie like a hawk."

"Can they check the DNA samples while we're on the ship? So we can get out of here?" Kallie asked, hopefully.

Tess was sitting on a nearby couch, waiting, and she waved and joined them.

"What, you want to leave the ship? But it's so

nice staring at the same walls for seven days," Reilly replied, teasingly. "We don't have that kind of complicated equipment on board. To be honest, we've never needed it until this trip."

"Then why are they—?"

Reilly glanced back to make sure the agent wasn't coming to harass them, then seemed to relax into the subject that he knew so well. "He could use it to get a warrant, or for extradition, maybe – if the samples can be tested here in Cozumel. But I think he just wants the killer to flinch. That's not a bad strategy."

"Oh, because if someone refuses to give a sample—"

"Guilt isn't the only reason to refuse, of course. Plenty of people are conspiracy theorists about DNA. Or they don't trust the government, or the technology – or they're just private people who don't want their name in the news. And then on the other hand, the killer might be pretty sure he didn't leave a trace and give the sample anyway." Reilly shrugged. "It's not a perfect plan, but it's definitely worked before."

"He was rude to us – and *really* rude to Devin's widow," Tess told him.

"He was rude to Officer Reilly too," Kallie told Tess. "I think it's his reason for living."

"Charming. Well, I'm glad he has a hobby," Tess replied, sarcasm returning to her voice. She added with a playful grin, "Have you decided to help us solve the murder, Officer Reilly? Since *that* guy is destined for failure?"

"You two and your amateur sleuthing," he laughed, but squinted at them suspiciously, like he wasn't sure if it was a joke anymore. "I'm not writing off Agent Paul's abilities, even if his personality is less than stellar. But if you come up with any clues you want to share, *I* certainly won't ignore them."

Chapter Eleven

"Do you want to try the miniature golf now?" Tess asked, after they said goodbye to Reilly and headed back out into the cheerful sunshine. "The rain stopped, and maybe it will be less crowded, with so many people being interviewed."

"Sure, let's stop in and see," Kallie agreed.

As they approached the stairs down to the lower deck – which housed the putt-putt golf course and the upper end of the zip lines – they ran into a bunch of kids surrounding what looked like a pop-up trivia game. Edging around the crowd, they heard a teenage boy yell, "The School Bus!"

Red and yellow lights flashed brilliantly, and a nearly deafening siren screamed, as the boy apparently found out that was the wrong answer. A huge nozzle shot a wave of green gooey slime all over the kid, and drenched Kallie in the process.

"Oh, *gross!*" she moaned, impatiently brushing her disheveled, greenish hair out of her face – as the crowd of kids cheered for her. "Was that supposed to be fun?"

Tess laughed and hugged her best friend cautiously, avoiding the slime. "I think if you're seven, it's probably amazing. And I'm sure it will wash out."

"I just took a shower. Now I have to go wash my hair again," Kallie sighed.

"Go on back to the room, and I'll bring up some hummus and chips from the buffet. We're going to be late for the early dinner service, and I'm starving. Those scrambled eggs feel like they happened a week ago." She looked at her watch and frowned. "We're already pretty late. I'll see if Laura and Missy are out of their interview and tell them not to wait for us."

Kallie turned back toward the lobby with a pout, pushing her hair away from her eyes again and hoping the gunk would wash out. Surely they wouldn't use anything permanent on kids – their mothers would be livid if they had to buy new clothes or special shampoo at a huge markup so far from shore.

She was just getting onto the elevator and had hit her floor button, when a man in a stylish teal shirt and navy jacket ran up and blocked the door.

"Sorry," he mumbled, stepping into the car. "Oh, wow – *sorry*," he repeated when he looked closer, and noticed her hair.

Kallie's lower lip trembled, and her eyes teared up at the way he was looking at her.

"Hey, no. Don't cry. My sister's kids got hit with that stuff on our last trip, and it washed right out. I *swear*!"

She couldn't help but laugh. "Do I look that pitiful?"

"Uh, right this second?" he answered, eyebrows lifted awkwardly.

"Yeah, on second thought – don't answer that."

He reached over and hit the fourth-floor button. "Can you believe this lockdown? I hope they give us a refund or something."

"I thought at first they were going to keep us all locked in the restaurant together until they figured it out. At least now we're free to... well, free to get coated in slime, I guess." She looked at her reflection in the mirrored ceiling of the elevator and groaned. "Maybe I should've counted my blessings when we were locked in the restaurant."

"What's it all about, anyway?" he asked.

Kallie wasn't sure what to say, but no one had told her to keep the interviews a secret or anything. After a moment's thought, she replied, "Someone was killed on the first night of the cruise." She hoped she didn't sound gossipy.

"*What?!* Did they fall overboard?"

"No, um, the police think he was murdered, actually. You didn't hear?"

"No. Oh, wow. Nobody told us. I'm here with a group of old college buddies– I should ask them. Maybe one of them knew and didn't tell the rest of us." He paused and his brow furrowed in annoyance for a second. "That wouldn't surprise me at all, actually."

"Really?"

"It's an odd group. Anyway, this is my floor. I'm Gary, by the way."

"Kallie," she replied.

"I'm in 418, if you want to talk or anything."

Kallie recalled Tess's vow about not making eye contact with any men on board, but she thanked him anyway. After their recent wild experiences, you never knew when you'd need an ally.

* * * * *

The elevator doors closed, and Kallie suddenly wondered if the guy had been flirting with her. Surely not. She was covered in slime, after all. And who would hook up with some random guy on a ship? Didn't most people go on cruises with their spouses and families?

Well, we know one woman who had dinner with a stranger on a cruise, she thought to herself. *But surely Elevator Guy is less of a jerk than Laura's awful date.*

The elevator dinged again, and she got off on her floor, getting her bearings before starting the walk to her room. Letting herself into their suite, she made a

171

beeline to the bathroom and surveyed the damage to her hair. She looked like she'd been dragged out of a radioactive sewer, but the green color wasn't awful on her complexion, she thought with a laugh. *If I ever decide to go punk, I'll know what hair color to choose.*

She turned on the shower and went to pick out a change of clothes while the water got hot. Surely the onboard dry cleaners would have something to get this nasty stuff out of her sundress. She wondered if they'd bill her for it. *Probably.* She'd wait to see how difficult it was to get out of her hair. If Tess was right, maybe her dress could be washed in the sink instead.

Jumping in the shower, Kallie found that the slime washed out pretty easily. Most of it came out before she even used shampoo, and the last of it rinsed away as lime-green suds. While she was conditioning, she heard Tess come into the outer room.

"Hey Tess, you were right. It's washing out pretty easily."

No reply, but maybe she hadn't heard. Or maybe she was busy eating the hummus and chips that she'd promised to bring back to the room.

"I'm starving! We'll have to go find something besides that hummus," she called out. "I hate to sound basic, but I'd love some pizza."

Kallie quickly shaved her legs, rinsed her hair, and turned off the water. Wrapping a towel around her hair and dressing in a complimentary fluffy bathrobe, she opened the bathroom door.

"What do you think about pizza, Te–?"

She stopped in the doorway, dumbstruck. The room was trashed. Every drawer had been pulled out of the dresser, and the blankets and sheets were strewn about on the floor. Their dresses were pulled off the hangers and piled up in the closet. Even the mini fridge and microwave were sitting open.

"What the–"

The suite door opened again, and Kallie almost screamed, clutching her bathrobe and looking for something heavy to use as a defensive weapon.

"Kallie! What happened?!" Tess looked just as shocked as Kallie had been.

"I was in the shower..."

"And a Tasmanian Devil came in?"

"Apparently," Kallie replied with a choked laugh. Tess had always used humor to confront her fears, so she knew her best friend was just as scared as she was. Suddenly fighting tears, she slumped against the bathroom door frame, and Tess hugged her.

"I'm so glad you're okay. I can't believe this is happening again. Put on some clothes, and I'll take pictures of this disaster. It looks like we're going to be talking to security *again*."

* * * * *

Officer Reilly let out a long, low whistle when Kallie opened the door. "Isolated tornado?"

"*Very* isolated," Tess agreed.

"Wow, are you two okay? What happened?"

"Kallie came up to take a quick shower, after a close encounter with the slime machine downstairs—"

"Oh, I hate that thing," Reilly mumbled.

"And someone broke in while she was washing her hair."

Reilly walked around the room, checking the damage. "It doesn't look like they destroyed anything. Do you think they were looking for something?"

Kallie and Tess made eye contact for a second and came to a silent conclusion. Picking up her purse from the bar counter, Tess sighed and removed the nearly-shredded documents. "We think they might have been looking for these."

Reilly's eyes grew serious, but he didn't reach for the possible evidence. He looked suspiciously at Tess and then back at the papers. "And what would *those* be?"

"We're not exactly sure," Tess began. "They're letters, but we're not sure from whom. We found them, uh... For right now, let's just say we found them."

Reilly closed his eyes and rolled his head back in annoyance.

"We couldn't tell what they were, at first," Tess continued, faster. "We just grabbed them so they wouldn't get lost. And we knew that jerk of a federal agent would ignore us if we tried to turn them over. We were going to finish reading them and see if they were important."

"Important enough for someone to break into a cruise ship suite, apparently," Reilly agreed with a sigh. "Can I look at them?"

Kallie and Tess exchanged another quick glance.

"Only if we can have them back,"Kallie replied, hopefully.

"You know, I had women just like you on my beat in Chicago, but most of them were elderly librarians who'd read too many murder mysteries. A few of them were awfully helpful, though, at times. Good watchers." Reilly considered for a moment, then agreed, "You can have them back. For *now*. But I'm taking photos and I'll come back for the originals later tonight if they turn out to be important." After a brief pause, he added, "Only because I trust you."

"Deal?" Tess asked Kallie, who nodded stoically.

"Deal, but only if you listen to us."

Reilly's face clouded up again, but he nodded. "Deal."

Tess cautiously handed over the papers, and Reilly sat down to read them. There were a dozen undamaged pages remaining, but he read them thoroughly, frowning in some places and sighing in others.

"We think it's a letter to the judge who presided over a case that Devin prosecuted," Kallie suggested, when he'd finished. "A photocopy of the original, probably."

"I agree," Reilly nodded, grudgingly. "It sounds like the writer had some proof that evidence in the case was either doctored or downright faked."

"Actually, I was thinking about it while we were waiting *forever* to be interviewed, and I might know which case it was," Tess replied. "I can't look it up online to verify, but maybe you can check, Officer Reilly. It was on the crime blogs a few years ago. There was a local company that made a bunch of popular, cool outdoor toys for kids – high-volume squirt guns and trampoline boots and stuff. They invented these funny shoes where you could glide over the water on floating platforms – but they got in trouble when some adult got drunk and tried to use them at the beach during a tropical storm. There was a big lawsuit, even though the instructions said there was a 125-pound weight limit and that it required a lifejacket and adult supervision."

"Why do you think it's that particular case?" Reilly asked, curiously.

"This line about 'fat, drunk idiot' in the letter got me wondering, and I recalled that the company in this case received an unusually harsh sentence, even though it was an accidental death case. There was a lot of buzz about it at the time, because it seemed unjust – especially when the warnings were so obviously ignored."

"Water Walkers," Kallie mumbled.

Tess and Reilly glanced over at Kallie, confused.

"They were called Water Walkers. And I may or may not have gone on a diet to get below the weight limit when they were first released, because they were so cool." Kallie looked back at them and shrugged. "I'm admitting nothing, but I can confirm that the instructions also suggested a bike helmet."

Tess grinned at Kallie for a second and shook her head before continuing, "But the letter implies that the drowning victim's toxicology evidence was faked by Devin, and some of the company's extensive safety testing evidence was destroyed in what the author calls a suspicious fire. That's a huge accusation."

"I wondered if Devin's murder meant that the judge received this letter and chose to ignore it," Kallie mused aloud. "But I didn't see any proof in there that it was ever mailed."

Reilly skipped to the next page and stopped again. "Wow. It also says that Devin told the jury outright to 'punish corporate greed' and asks why the judge didn't question that kind of vigilantism in court. I wonder if the guy was the judge's nephew or something. I mean, 'corporate greed?' It sounds like they were just a mom-and-pop company that was lucky enough to get picked up by a toy distributor – not Enron."

"I remember that was suggested on the blogs at the time, actually. But nobody found an obvious connection between the judge and the deceased," Tess added.

"If the killer lost his wife but *still* tried to do the right thing, pleading with the judge to reconsider – and was ignored – that could've triggered him to handle it the wrong way," Kallie agreed.

Reilly continued reading, but when he reached the last two pages, his forehead wrinkled in curiosity and concern. "The letter definitely sounds like it's from the killer, but the last page looks like someone's travel itinerary. You found these papers on the ship, right?" He took out his phone and quickly photographed the last two pages.

Kallie nodded, moving over to look at the last page. "I didn't notice the last pages were different; we were in such a hurry—" She shut her mouth abruptly and changed the subject. "Uh, do you think it's the killer's itinerary?"

"It could belong to anyone," Reilly answered, flipping between the pages again. "There's no name on it, and it's only for the last two days of the cruise. But in the context of these other pages, it's probably either the killer's or the victim's schedule."

"Anything sinister planned for those days?" Kallie asked. "A scheduled visit to a voodoo priestess or an abandoned cemetery, maybe?"

"Only the usual, I'm afraid," Reilly answered with a smile. "But I can compare it with Devin's schedule and see if it was his. If so, then the itinerary was probably only used for advance planning. The killer had obviously already succeeded in his intent, so the rest of his plans won't tell us much."

Kallie nodded and leaned back against the couch in exhaustion and disappointment.

"Hang on, there's something in here between the judge's letter and the itinerary," Reilly noted. He fiddled with the pages until he got them separated. "There's an extra half sheet of notebook paper in here. It's a..." He read the small document with an unpleasant scowl. "I guess you'd call it a poem? The kind you read in school, where the lines don't rhyme? It's a bit... dark."

"Really?" Tess asked, as she and Kallie each crowded around Reilly to read the newly discovered page. A few lines were scrawled in a cramped narrow hand:

> *Lonely days, desperate nights*
>
> *Lost without my love*
>
> *Sandy shores of loneliness*
>
> *So many people drown at sea*

"It's not very good," Kallie mumbled, and then quickly put her hand over her mouth in embarrassment. "Oh, I didn't mean to criticize his trauma—"

"Even a 13-year-old goth girl would call that a little melodramatic, Kal," Tess answered gently. "But at least his message is crystal clear."

"It is pretty grim," Reilly agreed. "This last part about 'so many people drown at sea,' though. I wonder if that's about the accident from the lawsuit, or—?"

Kallie and Tess both looked at him curiously.

Reilly hesitated, looked at them thoughtfully, but then sighed and shook his head. "I can't. Honestly, you girls seem smart enough to solve this. Certainly smarter than that Fed—"

Kallie nodded, hoping she looked encouraging but not pushy.

I know you want to tell us. We can help you—

"But I can't risk my job. I retired from the force to take this position, and the board of directors wants to keep it quiet."

Now Tess was nodding too, but she replied, "We understand..."

"If it caused a scandal, and I was involved—"

"No, don't risk your career," Kallie added, sincerely.

"Besides, I'm sure we can weasel it out of

someone else," Tess teased, with a smile.

Reilly laughed. "I have no doubt. And I'm sure someone will spill the beans."

"And you think the mysterious thing you can't tell us is related to this letter?" Kallie asked.

"Not yet, but I'm willing to look into it," he concluded. "And I'll pull the security footage from this section of the ship, as soon as I get back downstairs, and see if we can identify your burglar."

Kallie took the change of subject as a definitive end to the matter. "Okay, thanks."

"And I'm putting a security detail on this hallway – no more discussion," Reilly added, now completely serious again.

Tess and Kallie both nodded, no longer in the mood to argue about being protected.

"Good," Reilly replied to their silence. "It will probably take an hour or two to get it arranged, but the guards will be here by the time you get back from dinner."

He took a dozen more photos with his phone and then grudgingly handed the papers back to Tess, as promised. Thanking them again, he left them to clean up the minor disaster.

* * * * *

"Hey, Tess. What's this?" Kallie asked after they'd surveyed the damage.

"What's *what*?"

Kallie bent down and pulled at a piece of paper that was sticking out from under the haphazard pile of sheets and blankets on the floor. When it slid out, she stood up and paused, looking at it, then held it out to Tess. "It's some kind of receipt. But it's only the top part, with the printed numbers. Is it yours?"

Tess took the cheap, tattered scrap of paper and frowned at it. "I don't think so. You found it *under* the pile of blankets?"

"Yeah. The intruder must've dropped it while he was looking for... whatever he was looking for."

Tess flipped it over, and looked at it closely in the light from the lamp. "I was hoping there'd be something identifiable. There's no business name or purchase notes or anything."

"Well, if we figure out where it came from, that number at the top will match some kind of record, right?"

"I guess. Can we get out of here now, please? I still feel like we're being watched."

"Me too, let's go," Kallie agreed.

She stuck the scrap of paper in her pocket and had just started to reach for the first of their multiple door locks, when there was another loud knock at the door. They both jumped, and Kallie let out a small, startled shriek, but when they checked the peephole it was only another security guard. They quickly let him inside.

The young guard looked much more serious than Reilly and a bit scary. He surveyed the damage, took at least two dozen more photos, and then checked every inch of the room, like he was a forensic investigator.

Which he probably was, in a previous job, Kallie reminded herself. *And he makes me feel more safely protected than that federal agent did.*

"We don't have any empty rooms, I'm afraid, or we'd let you move," he explained, quietly but without a hint of a smile. "But the chief is arranging to station guards on this hallway. Do you know what was taken?"

"We didn't see anything missing," Tess replied.

Not an actual lie, Kallie thought to herself, *because the papers had been with Tess*. But they really hadn't noticed anything taken.

"We'll know more after we clean up," Kallie added out loud.

"Of course," the guard agreed. "Let us know if you discover anything missing after it's all back in order."

* * * * *

"I still want to get out of here," Kallie complained after the guard left.

"Me too," Tess agreed. "But we need to get dressed for the late dinner service in an hour. Where should we go?"

"Let's just go listen to some music or something. I'm not in the mood for dancing, but maybe there's a jazz band in one of the smaller bars."

"Are you sure you're okay?" Tess asked, looking at Kallie closely.

Her friend laughed shakily, "No, not really. But I won't get any better sitting around here, waiting for some lunatic to come back. So let's get out until Reilly can get his guard stationed in the hallway."

"That sounds like a good idea," Tess agreed, looking a little nervous herself. "We can finish cleaning up this mess after dinner."

Making their way down to one of the entertainment areas of the ship, Kallie and Tess didn't find a live band – but there was a quiet bar playing a medley of Frank Sinatra songs.

"Perfect," Kallie sighed, picking a booth near the back, where they could hear more music and less talking.

Tess ordered shrimp cocktail and crab cakes, even though it wasn't long until dinner, and two diet cokes. Soon they were drowning their fears in cocktail sauce, as Old Blue Eyes crooned about Jupiter and

Mars.

"Do you want to talk about sleuthy stuff?" Tess asked, quietly.

"Maybe later," Kallie answered sadly, picking at a crab cake with her fork.

"How about pictures of Sherman?" her best friend suggested with a bigger smile. "I brought your phone."

Kallie perked up at that, and Tess handed her the phone, sliding the charging cord across the table in case she needed it.

"You're the best friend ever," Kallie sniffled, flipping through her photos and finally beginning to relax a little.

Tess watched her smiling and chuckling for a few minutes, and then casually asked, "Hey Kal, how much was that bathing suit?"

"Huh?" Kallie asked, still feeling warm and fuzzy about Sherman's pictures. She was confused by the subject change for a second. "Oh, um, seventy-five bucks, I think. It was actually on sale. Why? Was it too much?"

"No, of course not!" Tess answered quickly. "I'm the one who convinced you to buy it, remember? And it looks awesome on you." She smiled cheerfully at Kallie, but her best friend could sense a plan at work. There was a keen sparkle in her eyes as she added, "I just thought I might use the rest of that gift card."

"You just thought of something," Kallie smiled back. "What is it?"

"I'll tell you later; show me your pictures of Sherman."

* * * * *

As they started to change clothes for dinner, Kallie took off her cardigan, and she felt the paper in her pocket again, and pulled it back out.

"Shoot, I forgot all about this receipt," she sighed. "I'll run down and give it to Reilly, in case he needs it. If it's from the ship, maybe he'll know where it came from." She looked at it closely and flipped it over. Cheap pink and white paper with dark blue printed numbers at the top. "It reminds me of the receipts from that cute little sandwich shop in Palm Harbor."

Tess looked at the paper and shook her head. "They all look the same to me. Every company in the world probably buys the same brand of receipt books. But I think if it was from a restaurant, the name and phone number would have been printed at the top of each page."

"Yeah, good point. And if it's from some random store in Tampa, we'll never find it. So hopefully it belongs to someone onboard." She put the paper on top of the TV where it wouldn't get lost and set the remote control on top of it.

"But almost everything's free on the ship. Who would need a receipt?"

Kallie sighed, "Beats me." Spinning around to look at all of the damage and mess in the room, she grimaced and picked up a few of their dresses. "I'll get these hung up before I go see Reilly, so they don't get any more wrinkled."

Tess had separated the sheets and blankets from the rest of the mess, and was making the beds again. She refused to ask the housekeeper for help, even though it would've taken her a quarter of the time to do it perfectly while they were out.

Walking into the bathroom, Kallie whined, "Oh no, I forgot all about my sundress! That stupid slime has been drying on it all this time. I'm sure it's ruined." She held up the green, crusty mess that had been one of her favorite summer dresses – remembering how she'd thought it might be salvaged if she cleaned it quickly.

Maybe if I soak it in the tub overnight with some shampoo, it'll still clean up. Or I could—

"Hey, let me see that receipt again," Kallie suddenly called, leaning out of the bathroom door.

Tess picked up the receipt. "Did you figure out what it is?"

"I'll bet it's from the ship's laundry."

"Oh, of course! That makes perfect sense," Tess nodded. "That's just about the only place on board where you'd need a receipt. I'll bet that number matches the number pinned on someone's clothes."

"I'll bet you're right. Let's go get Reilly."

* * * * *

"Oh dear, it's the Nancy Drew Crew," Officer Reilly said with a chuckle as they stepped into his doorway. "Did you find us another suspect?"

"Actually, it might be a clue this time," Kallie replied sheepishly. She knew he was only teasing but still felt a little burned after being ignored by the federal agent.

Reilly turned away from his desk, though, ready to listen. "What did you find?"

Kallie held out the torn receipt, and he raised an eyebrow. "I found it when we were cleaning up the mess in our room earlier. It was under the blankets that had been tossed on the floor, but it's not ours."

Reilly removed a small plastic bag from a stack in his desk drawer and took the receipt fragment by the edge. Placing it in the bag, he asked, "Was anyone else in your room?"

"No one we *invited* – not in the last two days, except the housekeeper and you. We thought it might be from the laundry?"

Without replying, Reilly stood up and walked to the adjoining office. "Mariel, didn't you say that your husband had his uniform tailored?"

A woman's voice from the next room laughed. "He's been enjoying the ship's cuisine a little too much. Why do you ask?"

"You don't happen to have the receipt?"

"Sure, let me get my purse. The seamstress gave us a great deal, if you ever need any alterations." She walked into Kallie's line of sight as she handed Reilly her own receipt.

"Perfect match," he noted, holding up his colleague's receipt and the one in the small evidence bag. He handed back the example and thanked Mariel.

"I'll take this down to the laundry and see what they can tell me," Reilly assured Kallie and Tess. "With all of the writing torn off from the bottom section, we'll have to hope they track the serial number at the top. The new security team is stationed in your hallway now, but will you two *please* be careful?"

"We're trying, Officer Reilly," Kallie sighed. "Believe me, we're trying."

Chapter Twelve

"Do you want to sit alone tonight?" Tess asked, as they entered the restaurant. There were a few available tables, since they were running late.

"No, I still feel a little creepy-crawly," Kallie answered. "Let's find some nice folks to keep our minds off this whole day."

"No sooner said than done, my friend. I feel the same way. See any likely candidates?"

Everyone around them seemed to be laughing and carrying on loudly, and Kallie wasn't sure she was up for that level of hilarity. She turned to check the other side of the room, hoping for something a little more reserved.

"Excuse me," a woman's voice called from behind her.

As Kallie stopped to follow the sound, a man's voice added, "We have room, if you'd like to sit with us."

In her state of heightened nerves, Kallie almost declined, until she got a better look at the couple. They were both about her dad's age, with silver hair, tropical suntans, and joyful smiles. Kallie was instantly charmed.

Tess obviously had the same reaction to them, because she swept quickly over to their table and sat down, just as Kallie was saying, "Thank you, we'd like that."

"I didn't mean to be forward," the woman added, apprehensively. "You both looked a little exhausted."

"But not in a bad way," her husband added. "We just thought you could use a nice dinner and some company. Try this cornbread, it's really good."

"We had a stressful day," Kallie acknowledged, nodding, as she took a slab of warm cornbread from the basket on the table and stuck her knife into a small container of honey butter.

"That interview was a miserable way to start the day," the woman agreed. "But hopefully it will all be smooth sailing from here."

"Smooth sailing," her husband chuckled.

"You were in the interview room this morning, too?" Kallie asked.

"It was the first we'd heard of the murder. You'd think they'd announce that sort of thing – although I understand they don't want to create a panic."

"It sounds like they have it under control," her husband added. "The federal agent told us to just continue our vacation as if nothing had happened."

"He said there was nothing to worry about, because it wasn't random," she continued. "That's what they always say on the local news – the public isn't at risk because the crime wasn't random."

Tess, who was a fan of local crime bloggers, nodded in agreement.

"So we're just going on with our vacation. Maybe we'll actually be able to get off the ship this time," her husband added, making her laugh.

"We had tickets on this same cruise when we got married ten years ago," the woman explained, giving her husband a cute glance.

"Oh, and you're coming back again?" Kallie asked. "That's so romantic."

"No, there was a hurricane, and the cruise was cancelled," she answered with a rueful smile.

"It turns out only *rain* is good luck for your wedding. Not hurricanes," her husband added.

"Sounds like it was good luck for your *wedding*, just not your honeymoon," Kallie noted, logically. "After all, you're still married, ten years later. That must beat some kind of odds."

The couple looked at each other and smiled.

"That's a great point, actually," the wife replied. "Even our honeymoon wasn't bad. We missed the trip but ended up driving down to Key Largo and staying in a cute little motel on the beach for a few days."

"That sounds even better, actually," Tess concluded with a smile.

"We still go back there every spring," the husband added.

"So now you're trying again after ten years, and this time we're stuck on the ship?" Kallie asked.

"We get a little closer every time," the husband considered aloud. "Fifteen more years and a few more tickets – we might eventually make it to Mexico."

"Maybe we should consider flying next time?" the woman suggested to her husband.

"I'll write myself a note," he answered with a laugh. "But it's not so bad. We're together. And we're meeting nice folks again. Can we get you ladies a pair of piña coladas to toast our anniversary?"

"That's so sweet of you. We'd love that," they both agreed.

"And we might still make it onto an actual beach, yet," Kallie speculated, with a shrug.

"We both have our fingers crossed." The couple both held up their hands to show it, and grinned at each other. "You never know."

"Gross! Mom, they put black olives in my salad!" a voice called loudly, interrupting their conversation.

The four of them all looked over at a nearby table, where an exhausted-looking woman sat with two kids.

"Just pick them out, honey," the woman sighed.

"I can't, there's too many!"

"Here, let me do it." The woman took the salad and started picking what looked like a thousand black olive slices out of it, putting them on her own plate.

"Twenty bucks says he doesn't eat a single bite of the salad after she's done," Tess whispered.

"No bet," Kallie replied, stifling a giggle. "Have you ever seen a pre-teen boy eat a salad? On purpose?"

"To be fair, I hate black olives too," their tablemate whispered.

"My burger has onions on it," a girl at the same table whined loudly.

Her mother mumbled something that might have been a prayer or a threat, and kept picking at the black olives.

"Raw onions, Mom."

"I heard you, sweetie. Flag down the waitress when you see her, and we'll send it back."

"But I'm hungry *noowww*–"

Kallie groaned and tried to drown them out by shaking the ice in her glass. "Sherman eats whatever I give him, have I mentioned that lately?"

Tess choked back a laugh and shushed her. "I can't even imagine how hard this mess would be with a kid. Much less two." She rolled her eyes and added, "Even if they were well-mannered."

"One of the female security guards said they're holding extra events and activities for the kids, since they can't let anyone off the ship," the woman at their table mentioned. "Not just at the pool, but arts and crafts stuff, and dance-offs."

"That's smart. And it probably keeps the parents sane for a little while."

A few tables away, the waitress graciously took the offending burger back to the kitchen, leaving the fries behind so the grumpy child wouldn't starve. Kallie wondered if she'd just remove the onions and bring the same burger back – but she was absolutely certain the girl would sniff the plate for onion juice. That waitress didn't look like this was her first rodeo, so she surely knew it too.

"I want ice cream, Mom!" the boy, who hadn't touched his salad, as expected, whined loudly.

"You haven't eaten a single bite of your chicken nuggets," she replied, ignoring the untouched salad. "No ice cream until you eat some dinner. You know the rules."

"Twenty bucks says she folds and gets them each a sundae?" Tess tried again.

"No bet. She'll fold like a wet napkin. Over-under on five minutes?"

"Under."

* * * * *

Later that evening, Kallie stood on the upper deck watching the crowds at the Cozumel dock thin out, moody in the dim light. Several other ships had come and gone, unaware of the drama on one passing vessel.

Tired of watching the freedom of the happy locals on the shore, she walked around to the ocean side of the ship. The blackness of the sea was a shock, even for a beach girl like herself. The gulf view from Owhiro was dark, but there were always lights overhead, living so close to the cities of Tampa and St. Petersburg. Out here, the ocean was pure blackness, almost like the water had sucked the light out of the sky.

Kallie loved the mystery of it. Anything could be out there. Smaller boats, battened down for the night, carrying adventurous families or romantic couples. Scientists doing research in small vessels or even submersibles. Whales and dolphins and a billion fish. All invisible to her eyes in the darkness.

She blinked and stared, trying to make out a single speck of light in the distance. They were so close to land, there must be something. But she could see only stars and a few reflections.

Could the murderer be out there somewhere?

Could he have escaped? Not in a stolen lifeboat, of course – they were well-secured – but slipped overboard from a lower floor and been picked up by an accomplice? Wearing an emergency beacon, maybe? The coast guard would already know there was a murder, but a fishing boat might rescue someone, lost at sea, without becoming suspicious. Everyone knew the ocean could be treacherous.

Kallie knew she was getting carried away, but imagining these wild scenarios took her mind off the creep who had broken into their room. She reminded herself that she was lucky to be alive. If it was the killer who tossed their suite, he might have killed her just as easily as he'd murdered his previous, intended victim.

She thought about being murdered in the shower like Janet Leigh in the movie *Psycho* and considered bathing in her swimsuit for the rest of the trip.

"Hey, Kal!" Tess's voice piped up behind her. "How's the view?"

"Like a black cat on a tar road at midnight," Kallie answered, turning with a smile.

"It's pretty, though. Peaceful."

"Exactly what I was thinking," she replied, faking cheerfulness and pushing thoughts of Norman Bates out of her mind. "Peaceful. Ready to go dancing?"

* * * * *

After half an hour at the Diskoteko nightclub,

though, they gave up on dancing. The music wasn't bad, but after the stress of the afternoon, neither of them was in the mood to frolic.

"It's pretty late," Kallie noted. "Want to go get frozen yogurt before bed?"

"Why, whatever are you insinuating, Kalliope Brooks? That I would spend the evening spying on a fellow traveler, hoping to catch her in a seedy affair?" Tess answered with a laugh.

"Why, no. I was merely thinking that dessert would be a fine end to the evening, especially when a girl is parched from dancing."

"And if the romantic fro-yo encounter should happen to reveal itself?"

"Why, I would be shocked and appalled!" Kallie answered with mock sincerity, finally adding, "Babe."

"Then let's go, babe."

Kallie and Tess made their way to the popular frozen yogurt stand, where there was still a long line of customers at eleven o'clock. Neither of them had any genuine interest in busting Helen if she was having an affair, but they were both curious. Mostly, though, Kallie had just been craving chocolate with crushed graham crackers and M&Ms.

"Whoa, there she is," Tess whispered, peering ahead from their spot in the line, as Helen left the counter with her order.

"I didn't think we'd really catch them in the act," Kallie whispered back with a self-conscious laugh. A moment later, though, Skylar followed her mother's friend, with two waffle cones balanced in her hands. The girl was still dressed in her edgy clothes, but she was smiling radiantly and looked her own age.

"She's here with *Skylar*? Just the two of them?"

"That's actually really sweet. That poor kid needs a break," Kallie whispered, feeling a little guilty for snooping and trying not to stare at the pair.

"No kidding," Tess added. "I hope it's keeping her mind off of the tragedy for a little while."

"Sugar can work wonders, I always—"

Tess suddenly looked away from Kallie, turning her body abruptly. "Excuse me," she called to a passing customer. "That looks amazing. Do you mind if I ask what you ordered?"

As the customer turned toward them, Kallie was surprised to see that it was Helen. Tess had charmingly approached the widow's friend directly, as serenely as a master spy.

Honestly, Tess can talk to any stranger in a crowd and make them feel like they've been friends forever, Kallie thought to herself with wonder.

Helen smiled and answered, "It's kind of a Frankenstein flavor. It's blueberry frozen yogurt with caramel, strawberries, and brownie chunks. It sounds gross, but it's really good. I've been back to get more of it three nights in a row," she laughed.

Kallie's nose crinkled up at the description, but Tess replied, "I might have to try that, instead of my usual mango with raspberries. Mine sounds so boring now!"

"It's totally worth a try," Helen answered.

Before she could walk away, though, Tess added, "What kind did your daughter get?"

Wow, Tess. Smooth.

"Oh, Skylar's not my daughter – we're just travelling together. She always gets vanilla with gummy bears."

"Gummy bears are my favorite too," Kallie answered, with a smile at Skylar – briefly and unexpectedly thinking of Morrison chasing her down the sidewalk, to surprise her with his favorite sour variety of the squishy treat. "But they turn so hard when you freeze them, it feels like they'll break your teeth. I usually don't get them on frozen yogurt."

Skylar blushed, but answered with a grin, "They last longer that way."

"Aha, a girl after my own heart," Kallie answered, admiringly. "That's so smart!"

"My mom always gets plain vanilla with strawberry sauce," Skylar added with a shrug which telegraphed that this was the most unforgivably, impossibly, horribly dull choice in the world.

"But she always gets it in the fanciest waffle cone, dipped in white chocolate and rolled in butterscotch chips. So it's not *utterly boring*," Helen joked back at Skylar, who blushed but laughed again. "She's not feeling well tonight, so we're taking her cone back to the room."

"That's so nice of you. I'd hate to be sick on a cruise," Tess replied.

"Oh, she just had a bad day," Helen added quickly. "It's not that nasty cruise virus or anything. But, you know, we women have to stick together, right? Take care of each other."

"Absolutely," Kallie and Tess replied in unison and then laughed.

Helen put her arm around Skylar's shoulders, and they turned to go back to the elevators – back to Samantha, with her frozen yogurt.

"Are you sure that was a good idea?" Kallie whispered as the pair disappeared into the lobby. "Now we can't spy on them at the pool without them recognizing us."

"Sure we can," Tess whispered back. "We'll just have to be more subtle."

"Oh, great," Kallie sighed. "Because we're so good at that."

* * * * *

"That's so sweet of her to take Skylar out for a treat, to give her mother some alone time," Kallie noted sympathetically, after they sat down alone at a table on the moonlit ship's deck with their oversized desserts. "I'm sure Samantha has a lot to process."

"Skylar has a lot to work through, too. I'm sure she needed the break as much as her mom."

"Yeah, Helen seems like a good friend," Kallie agreed, and then was startled into silence as the other two chairs at their table were suddenly occupied.

"Wow, this place is even busier at midnight than during the day," Tess laughed, greeting their surprise guests, Laura and Missy. "Have you two been up this late every night?"

"No way," Missy laughed. "I like my sleep, even on vacation. But they're doing a Silent Disco on the lower deck tonight. We thought it sounded like fun."

"We were just heading over there when we noticed you two sitting here," Laura added. "Wanna come?"

Kallie had never attended a Silent Disco before – where everyone wore wireless headsets and danced to music that no one else could hear – but had often thought they sounded like slightly surreal fun. She looked at Tess, who nodded agreeably.

"Sure, let's go," Kallie answered with a smile. "Do we need a ticket?"

"No, but there are a limited number of headsets, so we wanted to get there early."

Tess and Kallie both picked up their frozen yogurt cups, ready to go dancing.

"We'll go on ahead and get four headsets," Tess told Kallie. "Will you go get us some bottled water before it starts?"

"That's a great idea, sure." Tess and Missy went ahead to the Silent Disco, and Kallie and Laura walked to a nearly abandoned soda stand to grab ice-cold bottles of water for all of them. It was still warm outside, and dancing in the humid sea air would be sweaty, even at night.

"So what have you two been doing?" Kallie asked, a few minutes later as they walked toward the lower deck.

"I'm kind of an exercise junkie," Laura answered, "so I'm spending too much time in the gym. Missy usually gets a massage while I'm busy with that. We're taking a golfing class tomorrow."

"They have golfing classes? That sounds pretty—"

Laura stopped suddenly and hissed, "Oh no, I don't want to see that guy."

Kallie looked around, unsure of who she meant, or what he looked like – and quickly spotted a man nearby, who looked familiar. "That's the guy who was such a jerk at dinner with you?"

"Yes," Laura groaned. "Don't make eye contact."

"I'm not–"

Laura grabbed Kallie's arm and roughly pulled her away.

"I'm not making eye contact, and stop grabbing at me." Kallie jerked her arm away, shocked that her new friend had clasped her wrist hard enough to leave a bruise. Standing in a corner near the stairs where they'd likely be out of sight, Kallie silently inspected the man who had startled her friend. After a moment, she remembered where she'd seen him before. "That's funny, I just talked to that guy in the elevator yesterday. He seemed pretty nice."

Laura snapped, "He's not ni–"

"Yes, I *heard* you. And I'm not making eye contact, and I don't need to be dragged around. What's *wrong* with you, Laura?"

Kallie immediately felt bad for the slight, but her new friend wasn't even listening. She was still anxiously trying to get away – and pushing Kallie along with her.

Once they were back in the internal hallway and safely out of view, Laura apologized. "I'm sorry, that guy just gives me the creeps."

Kallie rubbed her sore and reddened wrist, still a little annoyed. "I'm not interested in him, but I talked to him in the elevator, and he seemed nice enough. He said he was on the cruise with some old school friends, so maybe he's just trying to get away from a room full of smelly feet."

Laura didn't laugh at Kallie's joke and continued to cringe in a way that didn't seem like her. "It's not the way he acted at the restaurant, that was just ordinary rudeness." She paused again, flustered. "I can't explain it, there's just something about him…"

Kallie studied her for a second and then nodded. She might not know Laura well, but in her job as a bartender, she had encountered enough dangerous guys to trust a woman's gut instinct. "Okay, I get hunches, too. I believe you."

"Yeah, it's just a feeling, you know?"

"Yep, I trust a girl's creep-o-meter," Kallie assured her. "Let's get out of here."

They slipped back outside through the double doors and silently hurried after their friends – toward the safety of the crowded Silent Disco, leaving the offending stranger behind.

Chapter Thirteen

"Hey, Kal? Do you mind if we stop at that Internet Café, before we go out to the pool?" Tess asked the next morning, as they were finishing breakfast in their suite.

"Of course not," Kallie answered. "Is that where you wanted to use the rest of the gift card?"

"Well, yes..." Tess replied with a smirk. "But not in the way that you think."

"Not to check your email?"

"After we talked to Officer Reilly, I got to thinking," she began, as she collected their dishes and placed them back on the room service tray. "Most of the passengers on this ship are even more addicted to the internet than I am."

"I wouldn't say you're addicted, Tess. It's just a habit," Kallie interrupted, defensively. "You've done fine without it so far."

"I'll admit the first day or two were a struggle, but now I like it," Tess agreed. "But listen – I figure at least half of the passengers bought the data plan."

"I wouldn't be surprised," Kallie laughed. "I

think the top tier plan costs more than the actual cruise tickets – if you don't have a free luxury suite, of course – but I'm sure some people *have* to fit that into their budget."

"And now *everyone* knows about the murder..." Tess paused and waited.

Kallie sat down on the couch. "So anyone with a data plan has already emailed their families."

Tess nodded, silently.

"The secret's out," Kallie added, considering the implications. "Reilly's bosses must be tearing their hair out."

"No doubt," Tess agreed. "And I'll bet people on the mainland posted on social media, and maybe even blogged about it by now."

"But they don't know anything *we* don't know," Kallie sighed. "In fact, we'd know more than any of them, because we had a head start on..."

"Snooping?"

"Researching," Kallie amended. Then she added, in a deep, mock-serious voice, "Investigating."

Tess leaned forward and raised an eyebrow, "Maybe we know more than the other *passengers*, but—"

"You think the other employees went to the *press*?" Kallie whispered the last word with a hiss.

Tess tilted her head. "Not everyone retired from

a long career to work here. They don't have any loyalty, and they might get 'internet famous' for blowing the story wide open."

"That's definitely worth the last twenty-five bucks on your gift card," Kallie agreed. "But I don't think it'll buy us much time. It's pretty expensive. We could spend a little of our own money to buy some time, though."

"Nah," Tess shook her head. "We're not detectives – and the FBI is here, after all. They don't need our help – I'm just being nosy." She picked up an information card on the bureau, flipped it over, and read out loud, "Internet Café access costs ten dollars for fifteen minutes."

"Wow, that sure does make you appreciate the free Wi-Fi at the Lazy Gecko, doesn't it?"

"No kidding," Tess replied. "I think it's cheaper on the bigger cruise lines, but they definitely know when they have a captive audience. Anyway, if we have twenty-five dollars left on the gift card, that gives us..." She paused and did the math, "around thirty-seven minutes online."

"That's not too bad," Kallie replied with a shrug.

"I mean, I can spend that much time searching for a decent recipe on a Tuesday night," Tess laughed. "But this story is probably already blowing up at home. So that should be more than enough time to search the headlines and find out what Reilly's hiding."

"If they have fast internet," Kallie concluded.

Tess nodded with a sigh. "Exactly. This info card says they use the fastest satellite uplink available, but I'm sure it would've been much better when we were parked at Cozumel."

"We might as well go see," Kallie replied. "It's all free money, and we can't take it home with us. Plus, there's really not much else to buy out here – so it's no tragedy if we end up wasting it."

"And if we don't find anything, then we can just go back to gossiping with Missy and Laura, drinking mango smoothies, and hosing you down with SPF 1000 sunscreen."

"What if we find something important online?" Kallie asked, unsure of whether that would be a good thing or a bad thing.

"We'll worry about that after our thirty-seven minutes are up," Tess replied. "But it'd sure give us some leverage with Officer Reilly."

"Well, what are we waiting around here for, then?" Kallie responded, grabbing Tess's pool bag. "Let's go find that leak!"

* * * * *

"Hi, um, we won a gift card on this cruise..." Kallie explained to the desk clerk at SeaWideWeb, the onboard internet café, as Tess looked around at the computers.

"Oh, sure," the clerk answered with a smile. "A *lot* of people use their gift cards for internet access, although most of them just use their phones. I can look up your balance and let you know how much time you have."

Kallie gave him Tess's name, and he verified that they had twenty-two dollars left, which would allow them thirty-three minutes.

"How's the speed?" Tess asked, as she joined them at the counter.

"It's faster when we're at a port of call," the clerk explained, "but we have a customized page to show the actual current download and upload speeds in megabits per second, so you can decide when—"

Kallie tuned them out, knowing Tess would check the speed and decide if it was worth their money, or if they should wait.

"If you'd like to add a credit card, you can stay online for as long as you'd like," the clerk explained, a few minutes later. "Or if you just want to use up your gift card balance, I can set the browser to automatically disconnect from the uplink when your time's up."

"Oh, that's convenient," Tess answered, nodding.

"We have a lot of families with kids," the clerk responded, "and they don't want them in here all day, just because they won ten bucks in a contest at the pool."

"I'll bet," Tess replied with a smile. "We'd like that option, please. We just need to run a quick search."

"Great, you're at terminal four, and I'll just activate that for you." He clicked the mouse a few times, and then added, "The time will start automatically when you open the browser. And I can give you a two-minute warning at the end, if you'd like?"

"Yes, please," Kallie answered, as she and Tess walked toward the computer marked with a big red number 4. "That'd be perfect."

Tess sat down as Kallie dragged a second chair over from another desk, and a small countdown clock soon started in the bottom corner of the screen.

"Okay, let's try 'Cruise ship murder,'" Tess mumbled, typing in the browser's search engine. "Hopefully recent news will come up first."

Kallie leaned forward and read the results. "Nothing but movies and true crime stories on the first page. Do you think the cruise line is blocking anyone from posting online?"

"You sound like me," Tess laughed quietly. "They might be able to do some strategic filtering or monitoring onboard, I guess – but they couldn't stop it on the mainland. It probably just hasn't made the national news yet. Let me try a more specific search." Kallie watched as she typed 'HappySail Murder.'

"That's better," she agreed.

Tess clicked on half a dozen Florida news website links, opening them in new tabs, and read over them quickly, as the on-screen timer counted away the minutes. "These are about the murder, but they don't have many details. They don't even have the victim's name."

"That's weird," Kallie replied with a frown. "He's pretty famous."

"Oh, I'll bet the news stations want to verify with Devin's family before they publish anything," Tess recalled. "So they don't get sued out of existence. And his family's out here with us. Let me try social media instead."

Kallie nodded, glancing at the timer again.

Tess opened a few of the popular social media sites in more tabs, and did a quick visual scan. "There must not be enough posts yet, to trigger a trending topic. Nothing but gossip about singers, and some viral trend called 'The Pop Rocks Challenge.'"

Kallie smirked. "You don't think—?"

Tess rolled her eyes. "Pop Rocks and Pepsi. I guess every trend does eventually repeat itself."

"I'm getting acid reflux just thinking about it," Kallie replied, shaking her head. "We're running out of time. Maybe we should email Morrison and see if he knows anything?"

"That's not a bad idea, but he won't be able to email us back."

"Oh, yeah," Kallie sighed.

"Oh my gosh, what am I thinking?!" Tess suddenly hissed quietly, angrily, typing a website in the search bar. "I should've thought of this *first*!"

Their friend Hannah's website, 'Homicide in Paradise,' popped up on the screen.

"Of course!" Kallie sighed. "If anyone would have a contact at the Port of Tampa, it'd be Hannah."

Kallie and Tess had met the local Tampa blogger after the Owhiro Murder, and she'd been a great help in their research. Her book on the crime was a bestseller, and Kallie had even written a few posts after they'd become friends.

"Two minutes, ladies," the clerk called out from the counter.

"I wish we could email her!" Tess complained. "I'm sure she has the scoop."

"There's nothing at the top. Scroll down to the recent posts," Kallie insisted. "We don't even know if there was a leak yet. Let's see what she's been writing."

Tess scrolled down and scanned the historical links in the right sidebar. "Look, here they are. 'Murder at Sea,' and 'HappySail or DeadSail?'" She tapped a fingernail on the desk impatiently. "Here – 'Update on the HappySail Murder!'"

Kallie watched the on-screen clock, as the last seconds ticked down, and Tess quickly opened all of the links in new tabs. The countdown registered zero, and a cartoon padlock popped up and turned red.

"That's your thirty-three minutes," the clerk reminded them, walking over to their terminal.

"Oh no, we didn't get to read anything," Kallie moaned. "We were so close."

"I opened all of the links, so I can take pictures of each page if it comes to that," Tess whispered. "But let's just ask—"

The clerk joined them and apologized, "Sorry to cut you off, but it's all automated by the café timers. Did you get everything you needed?"

"I think so. Could we print these pages that I have open?" Tess asked, sweetly. "It should only take about five sheets."

"Oh, of course," the clerk answered, genially. "The satellite fee is the real expense, and you're already disconnected." He pointed at the screen over Tess's shoulder, indicating the padlock. "You should still be able to click the print button."

Tess sighed in relief and thanked him, and then turned back to the screen. A moment later, Kallie heard a printer in the corner whine to life. When Hannah's blog posts on the murder had finished printing – actually a total of eight pages – they collected them and thanked the clerk again.

"No problem," he chuckled. "Like I said, most people just send emails from their phones." He pointed at a narrow door in the wall and added, "There's a metric ton of paper in that closet. We don't have much traffic in here, except for some grandparents who want to read on a bigger screen – and I can't *remember* the last time anyone printed anything."

"Thanks, that's a huge help," Tess replied with a smile.

"Besides, you saved me from epic boredom, for a whole thirty-three minutes. I owe you one."

* * * * *

Ten minutes later, Kallie and Tess were stretched out on their now-usual lounge chairs by the pool, swapping the printed pages so they could each read Hannah's whole story.

"The first post, 'Murder at Sea,' is pretty much everything we already knew," Kallie began. "Actually a little less, because there's nothing about the poison. She mentions her source, without naming him, obviously, and it sounds like it's either someone who works at the Port of Tampa, or someone with the cruise line."

"Someone who'll be unemployed by the time we get back to Tampa," Tess mumbled. "The 'HappySail or DeadSail?' post mentions the poison and the needle, and more personal information on the Devins. Looks like there was some spicy fight at a party a few years ago."

"And her *friends* were happy to gossip about it to a blogger, right after her husband died," Kallie replied with a sigh. "My faith in humanity has PTSD, Tess."

Tess laughed quietly and picked up her next stack of pages. "Hannah might be unearthing the most horrific friends in the world, but she sure is a great investigator. Reilly wasn't going to let any of this slip." She finished reading the last blog entry printout, and then handed it over to Kallie with a whistle.

"'Update on the HappySail Murder!' Kallie read the title aloud, and then continued in silence. She flipped the page, read the last of it, and then whispered, "Whoa."

"I *know!*" Tess replied, shaking her head.

Kallie got up and dragged their lounge chairs closer together, so they could talk quietly. "Somebody tried to kill Devin on the first day, right there in the port?"

Tess took the papers back. "Her source says, 'There was an incident as the ship was leaving port. The ship's security team apparently chalked it up as an accident at the time, but a man bumped into Devin on the upper deck.'"

"Which sounds harmless enough," Kallie added with a nod.

"It says, 'The ship always lurches a bit as they pull away from the port, and the upper deck is usually packed for the 'bon voyage' event, so it looked like a clumsy stumble,'" Tess continued. "But a witness said the impact was enough to send Devin part-way over the railing. Someone in the crowd grabbed his arm and pulled him back to safety."

"That's crazy," Kallie whispered.

"He wasn't injured, so no worries," Tess added, sarcastically. "All well and good – until he was *murdered* that same night."

"But why would the killer try to knock him overboard -- after he went to all the trouble of getting the poison on board?" Kallie asked, confused.

"Beats me," Tess answered. "It might've been a spur-of-the-moment attempt, in anger. Or it might have been a complete coincidence. Unrelated."

"That's a big coincidence," Kallie grumbled.

"Too big, I think," Tess agreed with a nod. "But apparently they're spending a ton of resources on investigating it now. And maybe that shove was the murder plan all along. And when it failed, the killer was forced to resort to Plan B – a needle full of... I don't know – tequila? Or aftershave? Or, heck, I've heard you can kill someone with a needle full of air."

"So should we ask Officer Reilly about it?"

Tess hesitated for a second, but then shook her head. "No, if he knows we've been searching for details online, he'll clam up even more."

"He's been pretty honest with us so far – even if he couldn't tell us about this part."

"And I don't blame him," Tess frowned. "This story makes his team look pretty bad."

"They couldn't have known what would happen later," Kallie added.

"I know. But Reilly's probably feeling pretty touchy about it. Let's keep it quiet for now, and see what else we can find."

* * * * *

After some more discussion about Hannah's blog posts, Kallie and Tess accepted that they'd need to do more research before it made sense. Tess opened the Notes application on her phone and started writing down everything they knew, while Kallie went back to her magazines. She was just dozing off with the latest 'Starlet Wars' tabloid in her lounge chair – when Tess whispered, "What's Skylar drinking?"

"What?" Kallie jerked awake, alerted by the tone of Tess's question, and looked around. "Oh, I think it's just the blue raspberry lemonade," Kallie replied, glancing closer at the girl. "They had it in the restaurant."

"What *is it* with blue drinks?" Tess rolled her

eyes.

"I love blue drinks," Kallie reminded her friend. "And blue candy. Remember, we got that blue ice cream with the rainbow dinosaurs in it?"

"But *you're* a grown-up – albeit one making weird, immature choices–"

"Um, thanks?"

Tess laughed. "I mean, doesn't Skylar seem way too *cool* for a blue drink?"

The widow's daughter had been stoic and aloof the entire trip, barely showing any public sign of shock or sadness at her father's sudden death. This seemed uncharacteristically childlike. Tess had a point.

"She does, actually. She's dressed different, too." Kallie scanned the pool area quickly. "And why is she *all by herself*?"

The normally edgy girl was in plain shorts and a t-shirt, sitting alone with her drink, sideways on a lounge chair, and staring blankly at the ocean.

"Maybe she's processing her grief and just got past the denial stage." Tess answered absently, though Kallie saw that she was watching Skylar with barely concealed concern.

"I guess." Kallie felt guilty for staring at the young girl, like an anthropologist watching another species, and wondered where Skylar's mother and Helen were. "I don't think she should be alone."

"I don't either. But we can't talk to her, she'll think we're weirdos. Let's go ask a steward to check on her."

"I feel like we know her already, but she probably wouldn't even remember us. Poor kid," Kallie agreed, looking around again. "There goes one of the security team members. I'll ask her to check – maybe she can invite Skylar to play a game with the other kids or something."

Security had been increased after the murder, of course – as much as it was possible with the limited number of guards on the ship – and it seemed like there were even more of the protectors wherever the passengers' kids were congregated.

Kallie approached one of the young female guards, unsure of exactly what to say. "Um, hi. This is going to sound weird, but we're a little concerned about that young lady—"

The guard nodded in acknowledgement, "We're keeping an eye on her."

Oh, right. Officer Navarro pointed her out, after that rude outburst against Devin in the interview room, Kallie remembered, feeling awful for the girl again. *Everyone on board must know who Skylar is now. I'll bet she feels like an amoeba under a microscope.*

"She seems a little—"

"Out of it. It's normal, in her situation. We were

trying to let her work it out with her mom, but we're going to have a counselor step in." The guard looked right at Kallie for the first time and gave her a half-smile. "Thank you for noticing."

"Well, it takes a village, or whatever. I'm just glad you don't think we're crazy."

As they turned back toward the pool, to Kallie's surprise, Officer Reilly stepped up behind them.

"Can I speak with you?" he asked.

Uh oh. Maybe she did think we're crazy...

"Of course," Kallie answered, pulling Tess along with her as they moved away from the other guard. "Are we in trouble?"

"Not this time," he chuckled. "I pulled the video from outside your room, but the burglar was wearing a hoodie. We couldn't make out his face, and he has an average height and build. Not much help, I'm afraid."

Kallie's face fell.

"Oh, okay. Well, thank you for trying, Officer Reilly," Tess replied. After a moment, she added quietly, with a conspiratorial tone, "We found something a little *more* interesting, actually."

Subtle, Tess.

"Someone on my staff didn't want to keep their job, I take it?" Reilly asked, with a sigh.

"Actually, no," Kallie reassured him. "We didn't have to go that route."

"Oh, good," Reilly answered with a relieved smile.

Tess winced. "Not sure you're going to be so happy when you hear the rest. We found out about the incident on the upper deck. On the internet."

Reilly groaned and pressed his fingers to his temples, like he could manually fight off the incoming headache. "The internet?"

"I'm afraid so. Someone tried to kill Mr. Devin on the first day?"

"Have you told anyone else?" Reilly asked, eyes closed in dismay.

"No, of course not," Tess replied, looking a little surprised at the question.

Reilly raised a cautious eyebrow at Tess and asked, "Are you planning to send any information back to the press?"

"Absolutely not," Kallie answered, and then added with a head tilt, "I mean, we might collaborate on the true crime novel when it's all over—"

"Naturally," Reilly chuckled, roughly.

"But we would never leak anything, and risk making you and your team look bad," Tess added, sincerely.

"And besides, we're out of minutes," Kallie reassured him with a smile.

"I appreciate your candor and discretion," Reilly

replied. He looked like he might walk away, but apparently changed his mind. "I hope I don't live to regret this, but you've given me a lot of information... We retrieved our onboard video from the launch, where Devin was jostled. There was nothing from the ship's top deck security cameras, but one of the interviewed passengers happened to catch it, and she handed over the clip from her phone."

"Seriously? Some tourist caught him in the act?" Tess replied in awe.

"A grandmother from Duluth, Minnesota, in fact," Reilly answered. "She was filming her grandkids waving goodbye to the people on the dock, and got a perfect shot. And the shove was obviously intentional, too. The assailant really put his shoulder into it."

"You're *kidding*?! You caught the guy?" Kallie grinned.

"Our security muscle team went to his room earlier this morning – armed to the teeth, expecting a struggle – and they found him just snoozing away the day," Reilly told them, shaking his head in amazement. "Not a care in the world."

"Weird," Kallie responded. "Although, if he finally avenged his wife's death – or however he saw it – maybe he didn't have any worries left. Just feeling right with the universe."

"We'll find out. Agent Paul and I are going to interview him in the brig, in fifteen minutes," Reilly concluded.

"Like in Star Trek," Tess whispered, earning an elbow from Kallie.

"The ship will send out a formal announcement if he confesses, since all of the passengers have been affected now, but I'll try to keep you posted personally."

Chapter Fourteen

"Oh my goodness, I don't even know what to do with myself, now that there's no mystery to solve," Kallie laughed giddily, as they walked back into their luxurious suite – which looked peaceful and safe again, for a change.

With no crazed lunatic available to break in and steal anything else. Or kill us in our sleep for snooping.

And, oh look, my hands have stopped shaking, for the first time in four days.

"For starters, I'm calling the spa to book our massages again," Tess replied. "And we can finally leave the ship, even though we missed Cozumel completely."

"I'm sure there will be some kind of snorkeling excursion in Grand Cayman, even if we don't have time for much else."

"And we'll have actual sand under our toes," Tess added.

"Foreign sand," Kallie joked. "Not plain old beach-down-the-street Owhiro sand."

"Exactly." Tess grinned, and added facetiously,

"*Fancy* sand."

"And videochatting, and window shopping, and I want to try that conch stew," Kallie daydreamed for a moment of the next day's adventures. "And that poor family can get on an airplane and fly home. With a little bit of closure."

Tess nodded. "I hope so. Samantha and Skylar didn't do anything to deserve this, and they're the ones who are really paying for Devin's misdeeds – according to the letter, anyway."

"I was thinking of how trapped we've felt for the past twenty-four hours, and now I remember how awful it must've been for *them*."

"Okay, let's stop talking about it now," Tess replied. "The worst is over, and maybe we even helped Reilly catch the bad guy. Let's go get that pizza you mentioned and drink a toast to Officer Edmund Reilly and his mad cop skills."

"Good idea. Maybe he'll be able to join us for a few minutes after he gets that confession. I'm going to take a quick shower and change out of this scratchy dress."

And not even think for a single second about Norman Bates, this time.

"There are about thirty pizza places on board, so I'll find the best one in the cruise line's dining app while you're getting ready," Tess promised, reaching for her phone.

Tess and Kallie were laughing in a booth at Pizzeria Perfecto – the restaurant with the highest ratings for pizza slices on the ship – when they saw Reilly passing the doorway, with his colleague Mariel. Kallie jumped up to catch him.

"Officer Reilly," she called, and they both turned back toward her. "We were just talking about you. Want to join us for pizza and a toast?"

Reilly and Mariel glanced at each other for a second, looking a little ominous, and he walked back to the restaurant alone.

Don't be silly, Kalliope, he's probably just exhausted.

The chief officer caught up with her a moment later and slid into the booth, slumping against the red vinyl seat with a sigh. "I was going to come see you later."

"How did the interrogation go? Did he confess?" Tess asked, excitedly.

Reilly shrugged. "We were able to identify him from the video – and when we spoke to him, he even *admitted* that he wrote the letter you found. But he has an alibi for the whole night of the murder."

"Wait, *what?*" Tess and Kallie replied in unison,

227

smiles sliding off of their faces.

"And I mean *airtight*. He was in the doctor's office, sick as a dog, and he's on her office camera for every second of the evening. We had to take turns watching it, because he's a very *enthusiastic* vomiter."

"Oh my," Tess answered, with a sympathetic laugh.

"Hang on, hang on. So if he's not the murderer, but he really did *try* to kill Devin as the ship was leaving the port, and even got *caught* doing it–?" Kallie asked, confused. "That means someone *else* managed to kill him first?"

"Apparently," Reilly answered with an exhausted nod.

Wow, that's some serious karma.

"Or maybe he has a secret accomplice. But we verified that he boarded the ship alone," the officer added.

"Isn't it strange that he made the shove so obvious?" Tess asked. "Wouldn't it have been smarter to wait a few days and make it look like an accident out at sea? Or even better, a suicide?"

"I would've agreed with you, three days ago. But after reading that letter, I really don't think he cared about making it look accidental. Or about being caught. Or about anything except righting what he saw as a criminal injustice."

"I see," Kallie nodded with a sigh.

"We're still keeping an eye on him, of course, in case we determine he has a partner."

"Well, thank you for keeping us updated. We appreciate it." Behind the politeness, Kallie's stomach dropped – and the wave of fear and nausea, the one she'd thought was safely in the past, hit her again.

"There's one more thing, actually," Reilly added. "One of the room service staff recognized Devin."

"Okay—" Kallie replied, hesitantly.

"Not from the night of the murder, but from earlier that day. He ran into Devin in the hallway."

"Why is that imp—?"

"*Literally* ran into him, I mean. Devin was rushing up a hallway outside of the residential areas, and the attendant literally smashed into him, coming around the corner with a tray of used dishes. Plates and glasses everywhere, he said."

Tess and Kallie looked at each other quickly but said nothing.

Well, that explains the mess. Now just play it cool, Kalliope. You didn't do anything wrong.

"He thought it was odd at the time that someone would be down in the lower service corridors, but passengers get lost constantly in the first day or two. He didn't give it another thought, and he was nowhere near the actual murder scene."

Kallie nodded, hoping he'd go on.

"We were showing Devin's photograph to everyone on the staff, again, before Agent Paul's interviews, and I guess it finally clicked. He said he remembered Devin's face even though they only saw each other for a second – because it seemed so weird that he took off running down the hallway."

"What else is in that hallway? Do you know where he was going in such a hurry?" Kallie asked, trying to sound clueless.

And now I'm starting to realize just how clueless we really were... We had to antagonize two killers? One wasn't enough?

"The corridors down there crisscross the ship like a maze. The waiter was going to the kitchen, obviously, but Devin could have been going anywhere. Or he could have just been hopelessly lost and frustrated. We're still checking for any sign of him on the cameras down there, to figure out where he went."

Not too many cameras down there, please? Kallie hoped silently – not sure if she was more afraid of the real killer, or of Reilly finding them in the security camera archives.

"Well, thank you again for—"

"I don't know why I'm trusting you two with this information—"

"Quid pro quo, Officer Reilly," Tess answered with a laugh. "We promise to stay out of trouble."

"I'll believe that when I see it," he smiled in response, shaking his head.

* * * * *

"You know, Laura's really freaked out by that rude guy she met," Kallie mentioned to Tess, as they walked away from Officer Reilly, headed back to the pool.

"Hmm?" Tess asked, vaguely, not paying attention.

"I told you I met him in the elevator, right?"

"What? Who?" Tess finally realized they were on completely different wavelengths and turned to Kallie. "Sorry, I was still thinking about the lawyer running down the hallway. Who did you meet in the elevator?"

"That guy that met Laura for dinner. The rude guy. We saw him on the upper deck last night before the Silent Disco, and she was genuinely afraid of him."

"Really? I thought it was just a bad date."

"Me too," Kallie answered, still thinking about Laura's strange reaction. "She seemed like she was laughing it off that night. But she's a pretty level-headed woman, and I'd swear she was having a panic attack when she saw him."

"And then he got on the elevator?" Tess asked, trying to catch up with Kallie's story, as the glass doors to the pool deck opened in front of them and they stepped outside.

"No, he was on the elevator with *me* when I got hit by the slime."

"What?!"

"I think I told you, but we were dealing with the robber in our room, and... Anyway, he seemed nice. Really nice. And funny."

"Don't tell me you're interested in the jerk," Tess interjected with a scathing glare.

"What? Gross, no. I just meant that he seemed totally un-scary," Kallie explained. "Until I remembered, just a minute ago, that he didn't know there had been a murder."

"That's not unusual, Kal. Most of the people on the ship didn't know about the murder."

"He specifically told me that he hadn't heard about it and he'd have to ask his roommates. But we saw him in the crowd outside the buffet that night, remember?"

"Oh my gosh, that's *right*. Laura took off her heels, so she'd be less visible. I completely forgot about that," Tess groaned. "Could she have been mistaken?"

"I doubt it. She'd just seen him earlier that evening."

"Which means he'd be in Reilly's facial recognition group in that hallway. Security would have spoken to him right away."

"Which means he was lying to me in the elevator," Kallie added, still considering what it meant, as she sat down on a deck chair in the shade.

"There's probably a logical explanation—" Tess added, tentatively.

"Yeah, I just haven't come up with it yet. Why would he lie about it? It was only thirty seconds in an elevator. If he wanted to avoid a morbid subject, it's not like I was going to force him to talk about it," Kallie replied. "Like mandatory elevator therapy."

"Maybe Reilly and his team hadn't caught up with him yet?"

"I guess. But Laura's not a flighty, timid girl. If her intuition was telling her to run for the hills, maybe she solved this whole thing before any of us."

"Wait, you think he's the *killer*?" Tess asked. "What's his motive?"

"If the murder was based on one of Devin's lawsuits, and it wasn't the Water Walkers guy, then it could be literally anyone on the ship," Kallie admitted. "But if Laura's bad date is the killer, and he saw us downstairs near the conference room, and *then* met me on the elevator—"

"Then he could have just zipped right up the stairs and seen which room you went into," Tess finished her thought, with a look of horror on her face. "And since he saw you covered in slime, he knew you were going straight to the shower."

"Plenty of time to break in and search the room," Kallie agreed. "We might be completely paranoid, but it all adds up. Think it's worth having him checked out?"

"Definitely," Tess sighed. "We've already spent half this cruise with Officer Reilly. I'm sure we'll run into him again any second now."

"Get away from me, Bill. I don't want to see you right now," a woman's voice spoke from somewhere to the left of the pool, loudly but in a surprisingly calm tone. Kallie and Tess were both startled out of their conversation.

"But Margaret, it wasn't–"

"I said, get *away* from me, Bill." Slightly louder now. "Don't make me call security."

"If you'd just let me explain–"

"GET AWAY FROM ME!!" Security guards hurried toward the escalating sound. "I hate you! Stay away from me, and you can get your own room, if your floozy doesn't want you anymore."

Kallie looked at Tess, who was frowning with increasing alarm at the outburst.

The man moved back toward the woman, apparently hoping to plead his case, but the guards grabbed him by both arms and pulled him away.

"Let's just leave the lady alone for now, what do

you say?" the larger guard, a polite and well-tanned blonde, who was roughly the size of a silverback gorilla, requested. "She clearly isn't interested in your company at this time."

The man finally registered the presence of the guards, looked the uniformed Scandinavian giant up and down, and nodded in sensible agreement.

"Good choice, sir," The guard approved quietly.

They led him away casually, not manhandling him but keeping him on a straight and constant path away from the woman.

"Why couldn't we end up on a normal cruise, Kallie?" Tess moaned.

"I just had a horrible thought. What if this *is* normal?"

"Next time we're taking a canoe."

"A canoe and a masseuse," Kallie agreed. "That sounds like the perfect plan."

* * * * *

"Here's your iced tea," Daphne told Kallie. "And I'll have your iced chai up in just a minute." She was pretty busy, so they didn't hold her up with conversation.

A few minutes later, Tess reached for her chai and told the barista that they'd see her later.

Kallie sipped her frosty green tea and thought about the lady who had yelled at her husband earlier. "That lady was really mad. I wonder where her husband will sleep, since she's obviously not going to let him into their room?"

"I'm sure the cruise line has some kind of setup, since they don't have any available rooms. Maybe they have rollaway cots in the indoor basketball court or something."

"He could probably sleep on a lounge chair by the pool," Kallie considered. "I don't think they chase anyone away after a certain time, do they?"

"I'm not sure. I know they drain the pool every night, so maybe they put up some kind of barricade or ropes to keep people away, so they don't fall in and get hurt." Tess shrugged. "It might be safer to sleep on the miniature golf course."

* * * * *

When they went back to the deck for a stroll after dinner, though, they found that Bill had returned. And he'd apparently been rejected by his wife again.

"Dude, I can't believe she talked to you like that," another guy, who seemed to be a stranger, addressed the dejected man.

Bill looked at the interloping man for a moment,

seeming to have just noticed him, but didn't reply.

"There are tons of other fish in the sea, dude. You don't need her."

The man they knew only as Bill sighed, sat down on a lounge chair and dropped his face into his hands.

"Who yells at a guy like that? In public? You're better off without her crap, dude."

"We've been married for twelve years," Bill mumbled. "We have two kids."

The other guy didn't seem to hear him. He gestured toward the crowded poolside, stunningly lit for evening, flipping his long ponytail. "There's dozens of hot chicks right here on this boat, dude."

"I don't want a hot chick." He curled up in the fetal position against the back of the chair and wrapped his arms around his knees. "I just want my Maggie."

"Suit yourself, dude," the younger guy replied with a noisy laugh. "More for me!" He wandered off toward the pool to scope out the possibilities.

"And I wasn't with a 'floozy,' either," he muttered to himself, after his erstwhile therapist was gone.

"Poor Bill," Kallie whispered. "He sounds like he means it."

"Eh," Tess shrugged. "Couples get into fights when they're in stressful situations. And I'll bet this trip is generating some major cabin fever, too. They'll probably be fine tomorrow." But she looked concerned too.

"I mean, I don't want him sleeping in our room–"

"No, me neither–" Tess quickly agreed.

"But I hate to think of him drifting around the ship all night, especially when he seems so depressed."

"I wonder who she saw him with?"

"Who knows? Maybe just one of those pretty girls in the big musical show," Kallie suggested. "Guys never think of the consequences when they pose for a picture with a pretty girl."

"I hope that's it," Tess replied. "I'm getting all invested in this silly Margaret-and-Bill soap opera, and if there's actually a floozy, I'm going to be really mad."

Chapter Fifteen

"Oh, look, they have our photos back from the formal dinner," Kallie noted with interest as they approached the elevators and saw the photography desk set up. Then she added, sarcastically, "I wonder if I'm in any of them."

To Kallie's surprise, they were both in most of the shots. There were a few close-ups of Tess, but the drooling photographer seemed to understand his job – even while obsessing over the prettiest girl in the room. There were several adorable pictures that they both decided to order.

Missy and Laura were checking out their results too, along with a dozen other passengers. Missy leaned over Kallie's shoulder, pointed at one of the small sample pictures on the proof sheet and gushed, "This one is so cute of both of you!"

"That one *is* pretty cute," Kallie agreed. She and Tess had their arms around each other's shoulders and their heads together, and they were both smiling cheerfully. It certainly wasn't candid, but they both looked sun-kissed and genuinely happy. "And I'm not making a goofy face, for a change," she added.

"Shut up, you," Tess replied with a poke at Kallie's arm, as she leaned over to see the picture. "Nobody says mean things about my best friend – not even you. You look gorgeous."

"Exactly what I was going to say," Missy agreed. "It's too bad the photographer caught this weird guy in the background of your picture, but our brother is a graphic designer. We can get him to cut that guy out in five seconds."

Laura nodded. "He removed my ex-boyfriend from all of our beach photos."

Kallie was confused by their comments, and she looked at the small picture again, squinting closely. There *was* a man in the background, but he was far away, almost out in the hallway.

"I don't think it's that bad. But I may take you up on that offer once I see the full-sized version. I'm ordering it," Tess replied. "It's just too cute to skip."

"There are a few nice pictures of us too. Mom and Dad will want a copy of this one," Missy pointed out an adorable shot of the sisters posing with the captain next to an oversized wooden prop of a ship's wheel. "It's just the right degree of cheesy."

Laura laughed and agreed. "She'll tell everyone that we're best friends with the captain. I want this one, too," she held up a cute, smiling close-up of them at their table. They were both wearing fresh flowers in their hair and looked more like sisters than ever.

"Oh, make it two. That's a great one," Missy agreed.

"Aww, we'll get copies of that one too," Kallie agreed. "You two are so adorable."

* * * * *

"Oh, hey, Daphne," Tess greeted their friend cheerfully the next morning, as the elevator doors opened. "We were just coming down to see you!"

"I'm so sorry, I'm never late," the young barista replied, tying her apron strings behind her back in the elevator. "We had a problem with our hot water this morning, and I had to borrow our neighbor's shower."

"It must be so weird, living on the ship."

"It was strange for a while, but now I like it. I never even knew our neighbors' names when we lived in an apartment, but these neighbors are friendly enough to let me use their own shower."

Kallie thought for a moment, wondering if she'd have the nerve to ask her neighbors for permission to use their bathroom, much less their shower – and realized she'd rather suffer and wait for a repairman. And she'd had the same neighbors for years.

"I called the office," Daphne continued, pinning her name tag on her shirt as the elevator descended. "So they knew I'd be late, but they didn't have anyone available to replace me at the kiosk."

"Your smoothies are so good, there's probably a line waiting," Kallie replied, forgetting the girl's anxiety.

"Oh no, please don't say that–" Daphne moaned with worry.

"Ugh, I'm sorry. I meant it in the best possible way."

"If there are people waiting, they'll understand, I'm sure!" Tess added. "We've all had plumbing issues before. And it's not even 8:45 a.m. You're barely late."

As the elevator reached the Lido deck, they allowed Daphne to dash out first, apron strings flying behind her as she ran, and were relieved to see that there was only one couple at the kiosk. Kallie and Tess got in line behind the pair, who were too busy being cuddly with each other to even notice the slight delay.

"I'm so sorry," Daphne repeated to the couple. "I'll just set up really quick and–"

She froze at the door of her kiosk, eyes locked on the floor. Her mouth slowly opened like she wanted to say something, or possibly scream, but no sound came out. Kallie looked at her, confused – fearing she might be having a medical episode – and quickly stepped over to see if she was okay.

"Oh no," Kallie whispered when she reached the girl's side.

"What?" Tess asked, joining them. A moment

later, she added, "Oh, you've got to be kidding me."

"Come on, sweetie, let's get you out of here," Kallie whispered to the girl, with one arm protectively around her waist. Their new friend was already a nervous wreck, at the best of times, and this was far from the best. "We'll go find your husband."

Kallie moved Daphne away, back toward the elevators, as Tess explained to the other couple that the kiosk would be closed for the morning.

"I'll go get security," Tess added quietly. She stopped a guard at the nearby lobby entrance and explained that there had been another murder.

* * * * *

"Do either of you know this guy?" the young security guard asked brusquely, gesturing toward the body on the floor of the kiosk.

Tess was now hugging Daphne, who was still sobbing, but she replied, "No, I don't think so."

Kallie started to shake her head, but then looked closer and squinted in confusion. "Wait. Maybe. Isn't that the guy who was getting yelled at? Bill?"

Tess looked at her strangely. "I don't know who you're– Oh, *Bill*. As in 'Stay away from me, Bill.'"

"Yeah. I really only saw him for a second, when the guards were walking him away, but I think he was wearing those pink flowered shorts."

The guard was watching them silently but intently, like a viewer at a tennis tournament. When they stopped talking, he finally asked, "Does that mean you know him?"

"No, we don't *know* him. We couldn't really even see him, to be honest, but a woman was yelling at him near the pool yesterday. I think he called her Margaret. He was still out there after dinner."

A couple approached from the elevators and stopped next to Tess, asking, "Is the smoothie shop open today?"

The barista sobbed harder on Tess's shoulder, and Tess shook her head at them. *No.*

"Can you put a jacket or something over him?" Kallie asked with a sigh.

"The rest of the security team is coming, miss, and they'll bring the doctor. She has privacy screens," he explained. Then he stepped forward and spoke gently for the first time, "I texted your husband, Daphne. He'll be here any second now, to take you home." He touched the barista's arm, and she stopped crying long enough to acknowledge his kindness.

"I'm sure other people saw the fighting couple yesterday. They weren't sitting in our section, but they were very loud – I'm sure they drew a crowd. And two of your security guys intercepted them," Kallie explained.

"One of them was the size of Godzilla's nephew," Tess added quietly.

"Oh, that'd be Jensen," he nodded. "I'll check with him, thanks. You said their names were Bill and Margaret? We'll track down the wife for questioning."

He thanked them again and turned away to meet the rest of his team, while Tess and Kallie waited for Daphne's husband.

* * * * *

As soon as they returned to their suite, Tess immediately went to their coffee maker, pulled a pod from the rack, and started a cup of chamomile tea. Tapping her nails impatiently on the countertop until it finished, she carried it to Kallie and sat down next to her.

"Drink this. I'm sorry I don't have any honey – maybe if we'd ever gotten off the ship, we could've picked up a jar, like Daphne mentioned."

Kallie took a sip of the scalding tea and sighed, closing her eyes. "Thanks, Tess."

Don't think about poor Daphne right now, Kalliope. Or poor Bill. Or...

"Are you okay?"

"No, I want to go home," Kallie whispered, blinking the newly forming tears out of her eyes. "The way he was curled up in that little kiosk, Tess. It reminded me of—"

Poor Lex, we couldn't save her either.

"I know, sweetie. I thought of the same thing. Try not to think about it."

But the kiosk isn't yours, and the kiosk isn't in Owhiro. It's not the same.

Relax, Kalliope.

But her heart was still racing. "I'm trying," she answered with a forced smile and took another sip of tea.

"Do you want to go see Officer Reilly?"

"Yes, but I'm sure he's busy with the—"

"Yeah," Tess interrupted her so she wouldn't have to finish that gruesome sentence. "He'll probably be coming up to see *us*, this time."

* * * * *

It wasn't until lunch time that Reilly returned to their suite, ready with more questions.

"It's about time you got here, Officer Reilly," Kallie answered the door with a sympathetic jest, feeling a little better.

"It's been three hours. What kept you?" Tess added.

Officer Reilly smiled in visible relief at their good-natured kidding. "I wish everyone was as understanding as you young ladies," he sighed. "I've endured a lot of... unpleasant language this morning."

"You're just doing your job. Come on in, have a seat," Kallie stepped out of the way as he walked to his usual plush bar stool by the kitchenette.

"We do have some suspects – although I can't discuss them, of course," Reilly explained. "I had to interview them first, I'm afraid, before I could come talk to you. No offense intended."

"None taken!" Tess answered with a kind smile. "But we need you to reassure us – was he killed the same way as the first victim? I mean, it's the same killer, right? There aren't two murderers on board?"

"We don't think it's a second killer, but the cause of death wasn't the same." Reilly paused, clicking the end of his ballpoint pen for a moment, but then maintained his earlier decision to trust them. "We think the killer simply didn't have another syringe."

"Well, that makes sense," Kallie answered, surprised by the simplicity.

"His neck was broken," Reilly added, quietly.

"Oh, wow," Tess whispered in horror, as they both cringed. "That's really hard to do, right?"

"It's not something that your average citizen knows how to do, if that's what you mean. Not really something you can learn from a video on the internet," he continued. "It doesn't take a huge amount of strength, but it's a... *precise* skill."

"And we originally thought poisoning was a woman's mode of killing, but that wouldn't be—"

"Bill was a big guy. I feel safe in concluding that his killer wasn't a woman," Reilly noted, convincingly.

"Why wait so long after the first murder?" Tess asked. "Isn't that risky, now that everyone is looking for him?"

"We don't think it was planned. This victim probably saw something or stumbled onto a conversation and had to be silenced," Reilly suggested. He raised an eyebrow and added archly, "Or maybe he was poking around and trying to solve the murder himself."

Kallie felt woozy for a second, but didn't reply.

"Point taken," Tess answered, quietly. "We'll try to keep our noses clean and resist antagonizing the killer. So you have more questions for us?"

Reilly leaned back on the elegant bar stool. "Daphne Davis told me that you helped her and contacted the security team on her deck."

Kallie nodded, frowning at the thought. "We actually spoke with her in the elevator first. She was running a little late – that's why we were there when she discovered the body."

Kallie remembered Morrison teasing her about

tripping over a body during her vacation, at their pre-cruise breakfast, and again wished he was there.

How am I going to explain all this to Morrison? He'll never let me live it down.

"And you recognized the victim?" Reilly continued.

"Let's just say we recognized his *attire,*" Kallie replied. We don't know him. He and his wife created a small disturbance yesterday, so we saw him briefly. But he was wearing *memorable* shorts. I don't think I could pick him out of a lineup, but I could probably ID those technicolor pink shorts from orbit."

"The woman called him Bill," Tess added. "Did you verify that it was Bill in the kiosk?"

"Yes, his wife identified him," Reilly answered softly.

Ugh. That conversation can't ever get any easier, Kallie thought to herself.

"Does it sound like she killed him? She was pretty mad."

"Agent Paul is keeping an eye on her for now, but it sounds like she has an alibi – although it hasn't been verified yet. I was planning to walk over to the Salty Dog after I finish getting your story. Do you remember anything else?"

"He was still out by the pool after dinner," Tess added. "Or, I should say, he had *returned* to the pool, after your guys removed him from the earlier argument."

"This seems like an awfully big ship, but it gets pretty small when people are fighting. We try to separate them whenever possible – and sober them up as needed. Three-quarters of the time, that's all it takes to defuse the situation." Reilly sighed and added, "But then there's the other quarter."

"Some nosey guy was talking to him by the pool after dinner, lecturing him about 'other fish in the sea.'"

"Hmm, we'll need to talk to him too," Reilly answered with an appreciative nod. "Could you identify him?"

"No way," Kallie shook her head. "He was younger than Bill, and he had long brown hair in a ponytail – that's all I remember. But if you check with the single girls who were by the pool after dinner, they could probably *all* identify him."

"It looked like he was making the rounds – flirting grossly with all of them and hoping for the best," Tess added.

Reilly glowered. "We try to stop that too, but it can be hard to catch them in the act." He closed his notebook and thanked them for their help.

"Hey, one more thing we wanted to ask you about," Kallie interjected, before he could leave. "Um, our friend went on a date with a strange guy the other night—"

"Strange is putting it lightly," Tess mumbled.

"She said he made a big scene, called the maître d' a nasty name, and then got his butt kicked by the sommelier."

"Yes, I heard about that," Reilly nodded. "I wasn't there, but it made the breakfast chatter."

"Is, um... Is that guy on your list?" Kallie asked, hesitantly.

"For the murders? No, we have plenty of garden-variety horrific guests, I'm afraid. Rude, drunk, hostile, even violent. That doesn't get you added to the short list for... I guess it's looking like 'serial killer' now."

"Oh, jeez," Tess moaned. "I didn't think of that. Serial killer."

"Laura's a pretty sensible woman, Officer Reilly," Kallie continued. "And she's afraid of him. I thought she was going to have a panic attack when we saw him."

"We always keep a close eye on anyone who's detained during the trip, continuing up to and including the moment they disembark."

"So someone's watching him?" Kallie asked, hopefully.

"Him and a few other troublemakers. That's a big part of our job, Miss Brooks."

Kallie nodded. "I met him briefly, myself, and he

didn't seem dangerous, but I trust her judgment."

"Intuition is a funny thing. I can't rely on yours, but I definitely rely on *mine*. I'll check him out."

"Do you need his name? It was Gary something."

"Nope," he shook his head. "We have an active file."

"Thank you," Kallie replied with a sheepish smile.

"Don't thank me yet. I'm not adding him to the murder suspect list. But I can look a little deeper into his records and see if he's hiding anything. If he has a shady past, it'll be good for us to know."

Kallie nodded in reluctant acceptance.

"Oh, speaking of records," Reilly added, "we tracked down your laundry receipt."

"And you forgot until just now? That doesn't sound like good news."

"I took it to the onboard laundry last night, and they verified that it's their receipt," he explained. "Their system isn't really computerized, though. They want to install a professional dry cleaning software package, but the cruise line hasn't approved it yet. The one they want is pretty expensive."

"I had no idea there was an actual dry cleaning computer application," Kallie mumbled.

"Anyway, for now they're still using handwritten receipts and typing them into a simple laptop database when they have time," Reilly explained. "So it took a little while to research the serial number. They called me back today and gave me the name and room number of the woman who brought the clothes in for cleaning."

"A *woman*?" Tess asked.

"Was it Samantha Devin?" Kallie asked, growing more attentive.

"No, it was a woman from Chicago. She's on the trip with her husband and their teenage son. None of them were on our radar, related to the murder, but I stopped in to see them."

"Husband with a hard-luck lawsuit?" Tess asked hopefully.

"Teenage boy with a missing hoodie, actually," Reilly corrected her with a smile. "Tall, skinny kid. They went to see a live band in Tampa the night before the cruise left, and their clothes smelled like cigarette smoke. The mom said she hung up all of the newly cleaned clothes on a wardrobe cart to take them back to their room. But somewhere between the laundry and their room, the hoodie disappeared."

"Did the killer swipe them in the elevator?" Kallie asked, frustrated.

"That's what we thought, too. But she was in the elevator alone. We checked the cameras, but we didn't see when it vanished." Reilly shook his head in annoyance. "I'm guessing it just fell off the cart, and the killer had yet another *very* lucky day when he found it."

"Disgustingly lucky," Tess agreed. "Thank you for checking."

Reilly nodded, then folded his notebook closed and slid it into a pocket of his vest. "If that's all?"

"You're going to the bar to check out the alibi for Bill's wife, now?" Tess asked, with a slight smile.

Reilly surveyed them suspiciously. "That's my plan," he answered cautiously.

"Mind if we tag along?"

The head of security groaned and slumped against the back of the bar stool. "You really are two of those wanna-be amateur detectives, aren't you?"

Kallie opened her mouth to argue, but he held up his hand to stop her.

"Look, I can't lock you in this suite – although it suddenly sounds like a good idea. I can't stop you, but please try to remember that this is *actually* dangerous."

Kallie opened her mouth again, but he interrupted her.

"We already have two dead bodies in our morgue, Miss Brooks. You two have been helpful, and it was a kind thing you did for Daphne Davis. I'd rather not have to clean up *your* murders next."

Kallie nodded, silently.

"We promise to be careful, Officer Reilly," Tess

replied diplomatically.

"Which means you're planning to follow me to the Salty Dog." Reilly sighed, and then mumbled, "I swear, some days, I wish these rooms locked from the outside."

Chapter Sixteen

Tess and Kallie slipped quietly into a booth and ordered a pair of diet cokes and a basket of onion rings, while Officer Reilly spoke to a few of the Salty Dog's staff members. He flashed a photo to each of them and eventually found someone who had seen Bill's wife the night before. And *heard* her.

"Sure, she was here last night. She was trying to drown her sorrows," a pretty waitress told Reilly, looking at the photo and shaking her head at the news of another death on board.

"Great. That usually goes well."

"I think the bartender eventually had to cut her off. She's just a skinny little thing, you know. It wouldn't take much 'drowning' to knock her off a barstool."

"Was she sitting at the bar?"

"No, that was just a figure of speech, silly," the waitress waved a dismissive but flirtatious hand at his question and then pointed. "She was sitting in a booth near the back, by herself."

"So she could've slipped out of here, unnoticed?" Reilly asked, raising an eyebrow.

"I'm not sure about that. She was pretty mad at her husband, and she was telling anyone who would listen," she explained. "Loudly."

"You're saying she had a motive?"

"Actually, I was saying that most of the customers *would've* noticed if she left. And thanked the heavens for some blessed silence. She wasn't at one of my tables, but we could all hear her. She gave me a headache after fifteen minutes, and I'll bet I wasn't the only one," the waitress replied, rolling her eyes. "I'm not sure when she left, though. She was still there when my shift ended."

"Do you know whose table it was?" Reilly asked.

"Actually, no. We've been shuffling our shifts, since no one can leave the ship. We usually get breaks while the ship is in port, and we're a little understaffed to be covering 24-hour service. That's usually Mindy's table, but I know she wasn't here last night. You could check the chart in the kitchen."

"Thanks, I'll do that."

Kallie shook her head at Tess as they listened to Reilly's conversation intently. "Could this get any more complicated?"

"Sure, just wait for the next body," Tess replied with a sarcastic frown.

"Ugh, don't even say that."

"Since you could hear her," Reilly continued

with the waitress, "did you notice if she made any threats against her husband?"

"Oh, sure! I mean, that's what you do when your man steps out on you, right? But if I'd had to guess, I would've thought they'd find the floozy's dead body today, not his."

"Excuse me?" Reilly asked, sounding surprised.

"Sorry, the wife kept calling her that – the floozy. I don't know her real name. The girl who caught her husband's eye."

"Sure, but you said you thought we'd find *her* dead?"

"Yeah, the wife was angry, but she was pretty sad and weepy, too. And in my experience – and after three years in this job, I have a lot of experience – that's a lady who still wants the two-timer back. That usually means she's ready to take her anger out on the floozy. Er, on the seductress."

I hear you, girlfriend, Kallie thought to herself. *Another booze-slinging psychologist in training. Though the broken hearts in my bar don't usually end up in FBI custody.*

The detective smiled quirkily, but Kallie wasn't sure if he was considering the wife's guilt, or just amused that she'd used the word *seductress.*

"Thank you for your help," Reilly told the waitress. "Is it okay if I contact you with more questions?"

"Of course, sugar," she replied with a wink. "You come back any time."

Reilly blushed, but Kallie thought he looked cheered up by her friendly flirtation.

Tess wanted to leave after Reilly was finished with his interview, but Kallie convinced her to stay and order more food. The Salty Dog was a dark, cozy bar with tawny fittings and mahogany upholstery – nothing like the sun-drenched Lazy Gecko, but she liked it anyway. They ordered spicy chicken sandwiches and another basket of the fabulous onion rings.

There were about ten televisions on the walls, but it wasn't a typical sports bar. American football was playing on one screen, but two others were showing old black-and-white pirate movies. Kallie recognized Errol Flynn and Clark Gable among the charming old grainy scenes. The Princess Bride played on another display – there seemed to be a vaguely swashbuckling theme to the bar, but lighthearted.

After nostalgically watching Buttercup and Westley for a few minutes, Kallie looked at the other screens. "Oh, look. Some of them are showing videos from this cruise."

"That's a cute idea," Tess smiled. "There's everyone waving goodbye from the port. I wonder if they have hired videographers on board, or if these are from stationary cameras?"

"It looks like just a few cameras in the more

popular spots," Kallie responded, after watching the scenes change. "They aren't moving around. Is this all from the first day of the cruise?"

"I think so. There's a shot of the Skyway Bridge," Tess answered. "And there's some footage of people going down the big slide into the upper pool, which we never tried. We need to go up to the other pool tomorrow morning and try it before it gets crowded."

"Agreed, one hundred percent," Kallie replied. Then as the scene changed again, she added, "Oh, we haven't tried that dance club either. It looks popular, and I like those neon designs on the walls."

"It looks fun, except for all of that confetti. I'd never get that out of my hair!"

"Wait, where did we see that gold and silver confetti before, Tess?" Kallie asked, gesturing at the screen with an onion ring.

"If the video's from the first day, then there were probably hundreds of people covered with it."

"Yeah, that's probably true," Kallie agreed with a nod. "I wouldn't want that stuff— Oh, my gosh. Is that—?"

Tess looked at Kallie quickly, shocked at the tone of her voice. "What?"

"Oh no, that's Laura's date. Gary."

"Where?" Tess asked, studying the screen.

"Right there in the front. That's him, in the

white shirt, and those must be his roommates."

"Are you sure?"

Kallie sighed grumpily. "Yes, I'm sure. I got a good look at him in the elevator. I can't believe he has an alibi too."

"We don't know that this is an alibi yet," Tess replied. "This is only fifteen seconds of footage."

"And we're going to see Reilly again, aren't we?"

Tess smiled awkwardly. "He's going to think we're stalking him, I swear."

* * * * *

"Looks like that guy stealing the knife from the restaurant had the right idea," Tess mentioned later that night, while taking off her mascara in front of the mirror.

They had just finished talking with Reilly, who'd verified that their latest suspect was, in fact, dancing wildly in the nightclub, covered in confetti, at the time of Devin's murder.

Kallie's stomach was tied in knots again. "No kidding. Now I wish we'd pinched a couple of them too."

"Maybe we should order steaks from room service and casually swipe the knives."

"Too late now," Kallie laughed. "I'm sure the

kitchen staff is counting every sharp object by hand, at this point. And probably keeping them under lock and key."

Tess washed her face and then walked over and plopped down on the couch with her feet up. "So what do we think happened in the first-floor hallway, Miss Poirot?"

"That seems to be the anchor to this whole thing, doesn't it?"

"But only if it was the *actual* killer who met him," Tess considered. "Not if it was the wanna-be killer who failed."

"And what kind of person has *two* complete strangers, both trying to kill him, on the same boat?"

"The kind who has a ton of enemies – he doesn't sound like the nicest guy. But since we know almost nothing about his personal life, we'd just be guessing about anything outside of his business dealings and lawsuits," Tess concluded, logically. "Are you still thinking slimy tryst?"

"Not anymore," Kallie shook her head. "Now I'm starting to think he was meeting a blackmailer. Someone he didn't even know was on the ship, until they surprised him when he was with his wife and kid. Because Reilly said he was *running* down the hall."

"Oh, so you think he was running angry, not running scared," Tess considered, tapping the carved wooden arm of the couch in thought. "Running toward something, not running away."

"If he was running away from someone, that person would've caught up with him when he smashed into the room service guy."

"Hmm, you might be right," Tess replied, considering the possibilities.

"Anyway, that's what I think. What about you? You think he was running *from* someone? That would certainly change things – if he'd just barely escaped from *another* attempt on his life," Kallie nodded. "But then why not tell security?"

"Because that would mean admitting to something... illegal?" Tess suggested. "Or humiliating, maybe?"

"Okay, something that would wreck his career? His reputation? Or maybe his marriage?" Kallie agreed. "But what?"

Chapter Seventeen

"I think we need to consider that this might be random," Kallie suggested the next morning, when she saw that Tess was awake.

"What?" Tess asked.

"Agent Paul is looking at this murder like it could only be someone in the family. Since that's what always happens on ships, he's obsessed with it. He can't see past the wife and daughter."

Tess nodded, barely visible in the dim room.

"And *we've* been looking at it like someone else he knew in his day-to-day life must've bought a cruise ticket and killed him. A distraught defendant or a client, or the husband of a mistress."

Tess nodded again. "Those are the most likely attackers..."

"But what if someone on the ship just snapped? A total stranger?"

"Someone random and unrelated, who just happened to have a hypodermic needle full of poison in their carry-on bag?" The sarcasm crept into Tess's voice.

"I don't have the answers, I'm just suggesting a possibility. Lots of people carry needles for insulin and other medications. And practically everything's poisonous, if you jab it into someone's leg."

"Okay, that's a reasonable point," Tess agreed, fighting a yawn. "But the shredded letters? And the receipt? And the key card?"

"The shredded letter came from the wrong suspect. And Reilly obviously doesn't think the receipt and the key card are legitimate clues..." Kallie sighed.

They sat in silence for a moment, until Tess finally replied, simply, "I do."

"I do too," Kallie agreed. "But what if the break-in was just a robbery attempt? What if someone thought we were rich, since we're in this gorgeous suite, and they assumed we'd have jewelry and cash? Or if they just had the wrong room?"

"It wasn't. If we'd stayed out of this mess, like we planned, I could believe it was a coincidence. But we could hear someone chasing us down the hallway and trying to open the conference room door. When the whole suite was torn apart – that wasn't a mistake."

"Okay," Kallie mumbled. "Okay, I'm convinced."

There was a strange swishing sound, and Tess sat up to look around. "Hey, there's an envelope by the door."

"Oh, did they finally announce the dead guy?" Kallie asked sarcastically.

"I doubt it. And I doubt they would've put that in a big brown envelope." She stretched enthusiastically and then walked over to the door.

"Is it a giant envelope full of anthrax?"

"Wow, you're in a mood today," Tess chuckled, crawling back into her bed. "Although that wouldn't be a total shock, after the past few days."

"So what is it? Are we expecting anything?"

"Oh, it's the photos from the big dinner," Tess replied, intrigued, as she pulled the full-size photos from the envelope.

"That was fast." Kallie looked over Tess's shoulder, but the bedside lamps were too dim to see any details. "Let's go sit by the windows." She opened the heavy drapes, letting in a blast of sunlight through the sliding glass doors.

"That's better," Tess agreed, plopping down into an armchair and holding up the first photo in the bright morning light.

Kallie hauled over another sturdy, plush armchair – a benefit of their cozy suite – and squinted at the picture. "This is a great picture of you. I'm making a weird face."

"That's because you wanted to kick the photographer."

"I can actually read that feeling in my face, here," Kallie mused, nodding. "I look like I'm about to throw a shoe at him."

"It's not a bad picture of you, really. You look pretty, just annoyed."

"Pretty annoyed."

"Exactly." Tess flipped to the next picture, a close-up where they were both laughing at the table. "Oh, this is a great picture of both of us. We should get more copies of this one, for our parents."

"Definitely," Kallie took out the reorder sheet from the envelope and checked the number from the back of the picture. "Three more?"

"Make it four," Tess replied with a nod.

The next picture was a candid of the two of them dancing, and it made them both laugh. "This is really cute," Kallie smiled. "I'm ordering another one of these. And here's that great one of us posing – I can't believe how well this one came out."

"Wait, but what's going on in the background?" Tess pointed at the left side of the frame.

"Huh? Let me see it." Kallie held it up close to the window and then remembered. "Oh, this is the picture that Missy and Laura were telling us to have digitally altered."

"That makes sense. This guy is totally in the shot. What's he even doing back there?"

It hadn't looked that bad in the small review copy, and truthfully, the man was far enough behind them that he wouldn't have spoiled the shot if he'd just been walking. But instead, he was crouched over a trashcan with one hand on the rim.

"Eww, is he puking?" Tess asked, squinting at the picture. "What a weirdo."

"It wasn't even the first night, when a few people were still getting seasick from the motion of the ship."

"Well, we've got the picture," Tess replied with a shrug. "We should do what Missy suggested and just have him digitally edited out. She said their brother could do it for us, right?"

"Hang on, is that—?"

"Hmm?" Tess asked, already looking at the next photo.

"I think that's the fro-yo guy," Kallie added with a frown.

"The guy that was hanging around Helen at the pool? Ugh, I knew he was a loser." Tess took the photo back and agreed. "That *is* him. He's still wearing that tacky shirt. I mean, an ironic tropical print is one thing, on a cruise, but that shirt is just ugly."

"And dirty. Did he wear it every day? And to the Captain's Dinner, too?"

"It's his signature shirt, babe," Tess joked caustically, rolling her eyes.

"And his signature smell, babe. But what is he doing in the trash can?" She looked closer, and then shook her head. "I don't think he's puking. It looks like he's trying to pull something out."

"That's even better," Tess smirked.

"Let's see if the photographer can get us the picture right before this," Kallie suggested with a distracted frown.

"What? *Why?*"

"I just want to see what he's doing."

"Kallie? Who cares about that loser? We'll just get him edited out."

"Look, he didn't drop his *Rolex* in there, Tess. I want to— Okay, fine. I just have a bad feeling about it."

"Oh," Tess answered with hesitation. "You know, your spooky intuition got us into a *lot* of trouble once."

"It's just a picture. One picture won't get us in trouble."

269

Chapter Eighteen

Finishing their room service breakfast and quickly throwing on sundresses over their bathing suits, Tess and Kallie stopped by the photographer's studio on their way down to the pool. He was already open, hoping to make more sales, and nearly tripped over his shoes when he saw Tess in the doorway.

"Hi," she said, adding a small wave to minimize his stare. "We were hoping to see a few more pictures."

"Of course," he answered. "Come in, come in."

Tess held up the envelope. "We've got some pictures that we really like, but we'd like to see a few more. Maybe the shots you got right before and after our favorite?"

"Oh, um, sure," the photographer agreed. "I usually only put the best ones on the display for orders, so you've probably got the best shots. But I keep everything for at least six months, so I still have all of the other pictures on the memory card."

"That would be so helpful," Tess replied, sweetly. Kallie knew she wasn't comfortable with flirting to get what she wanted, but she could at least be friendly.

Taking the photo from her, the photographer flipped it over to see the faintly printed number on the back. "A378," he mumbled to himself, and then slid around a few memory cards in a small porcelain tray. Picking one up with a nod, he slipped it into the reader.

Kallie and Tess looked over his shoulder as the photo list appeared on the screen, and he smiled blissfully for a second at the feminine scent of shampoo and suntan lotion around him.

"Here's A378, which you already have," he noted, becoming professional. "You wanted to see the pictures before and after it?"

"Yes, please," Tess answered, simply.

"Okay, so—" he clicked the arrows on the screen, to show the half dozen photos before the print they'd already received. "Here are the 'before' shots. I skipped these because they aren't as good. You're both looking away in this one. And in this one—"

Even he noticed when Kallie whispered to Tess, "Look."

He glanced back at the screen, but clearly didn't see anything special.

"Could you blow this one up, please?" Tess asked.

The photographer expanded the photo to full screen, and then slid his chair over to make room as they both leaned in. Kallie turned to Tess and whispered, "Is that—?"

"I know this is a weird question," Tess began with a coy smile, "but could you zoom in on that creepy-looking guy in the background?"

The photographer scrutinized the screen closely and chuckled. "You know, I didn't even notice him." He zoomed in closer, so the man in the background took up most of the screen, and then leaned in for a closer look too. "What's he doing?"

"That's what we're trying to figure out."

The photographer was suddenly very serious. "Was this guy bothering you? Because the cruise line has a zero-tolerance policy on harassment. I can use these photos to help you identify him, if you need—"

"He wasn't harassing us, exactly. We're just... what is he *doing*?"

"Let me check a few more frames – maybe there's a better shot," the photographer mumbled, less love-struck now and more intrigued by the background subject's strange behavior.

* * * * *

"Is Reilly coming?" Kallie asked, a little while later.

"Yeah, he's going to meet us here," Tess

answered. "Thanks, um…"

"Kevin," the photographer answered. "And don't thank me, this is the coolest thing I've gotten to work on in years. Don't get me wrong. The accommodations are amazing, but photographing drunk rich people gets old pretty fast."

"Sounds like it. Isn't there anything else to do out here?"

"I snorkel in some of the ports with an underwater camera and get cool shots of the fish and coral. And I take some pictures of the locals. That's the most fun, but I don't get that much time on land." He pulled out a few photos from a drawer full of file folders – one showing a wrinkled, wizened old man tying knots in a handmade fishing net. Another captured a young girl with braided hair in brightly colored clothing, carrying a school book bag.

"Wow, these are really good," Tess replied, admiring them with a vaguely quizzical expression on her face.

The photographer silently nodded his thanks. "Here's Officer Reilly. That was quick."

"I was just down on the next floor. And I suppose I should've known you two would be here," the officer answered, leaning on the door frame and raising an eyebrow at the girls. "What's up?"

"We wanted you to see this guy in our photos from the Captain's Dinner." Tess took out the photos from their envelope and showed Reilly the original they'd ordered.

"Did you find another suspect for our gallery of rogues?" he asked jokingly, taking the picture and squinting at it. After a moment, he frowned appropriately. "What's he *doing*?"

"That's exactly what we said," Tess answered with a laugh.

"About ten of us have asked that very question, so far," Kallie added. "It's starting to sound like an echo."

"And Kallie got the idea that we should come down here and check with your nice photographer."

Kallie noticed that Tess didn't mention how creepy he had seemed while on the job. He was actually pretty cool in person.

Reilly turned to Kevin, expectantly. "Did you find a better shot?' He paused for a moment, then added, "Am I correct in presuming there's a reason we care about this underdressed dumpster diver? You didn't just invite me here to chat?"

"I checked the shots immediately before and after that picture," Kevin replied. "But then I realized it'd be better to— Maybe you should just see for yourself."

He moved away from the desk so Reilly could get a look at the photo currently on the screen. Kallie and Tess were barely in this shot, and Kevin zoomed in on the background man.

"Ugh. Is he *really* taking something out of the trash? At the most elegant dinner of the whole trip?" Reilly winced.

"We actually think he's trying to shove something deeper into it. I made a sort of... digital flip book," Kevin explained cautiously. Kallie could tell he was trying to dumb down the technology for all of them, but she didn't complain. "When you watch all of the stills in sequence, you can see..."

He clicked the play button, and a choppy, imperfect little film on the computer screen started playing.

As the lovestruck photographer had taken multiple photos of Tess and Kallie that night, the background man, apparently oblivious, walked up to the bin, took something out of his pocket, and dropped it in the trash. He started to turn away, but then went back and shoved it deeper into the other waste.

Reilly frowned and his brow creased. "Okay, that's weird. And also gross. But still not criminal."

"Here's the close-up we wanted you to see," Kevin switched screens so Reilly could see the full-sized close-up. The man's hand had just come out of his pocket, and he was holding the item in clear view.

"Oh, sweet merciful—" Reilly whispered. "Is that—?"

"Yep. Surgical gloves," Kallie answered.

"Okay, I'll admit this looks bad, but there could be a million rational explanations," Reilly noted, now back to thinking calmly and logically, as usual. "Not the least of which being, he was politely picking up someone else's litter."

I knew it, he's shutting our suspicions down again, Kallie thought dejectedly.

"But—"

"No buts, Miss Brooks. I'm going to check him out," Reilly interrupted, to reassure them. "*Believe* me, he'll be investigated thoroughly. Because that's our *job*. But I'll need to identify him first. You don't happen to know him, I suppose?"

"No," they answered in unison.

"No, that would be too easy," Reilly sighed.

"We've seen him out at the pool, though. He calls everyone 'babe,' and..." Kallie hesitated.

"See, when you pause like that, Miss Brooks, I can already tell you've been reckless, and that makes me very nervous. Is this bad news or just gossip?"

"Both."

"*Go ahead*," Reilly groaned.

"We saw him with the victim's wife's friend."

Reilly shook his head in confusion. "Who?"

"The widow, Samantha Devin. Her best friend is on the cruise with them, in an adjoining suite," Tess explained. "Helen."

"Her husband gets seasick," Kallie added, and then immediately shut up.

Reilly took a deep breath and closed his eyes. "Okay, we're not going to discuss how you know that."

"We've seen them together a few times at the pool," Tess continued. "And the widow mentioned that they met at night, too. I think his first name might be Pete."

"I don't recognize him from these photos, but if he's been even loosely associated with the victim's family, then we probably already interviewed him in the first two days after the murder," Reilly assured them. "And *cleared* him," he added, pointedly.

Tess and Kallie nodded in understanding.

Reilly stood up from the photographer's computer desk. "In any case, I'll review our notes – and find him again, if necessary."

"Let me know if I can get you anything else," Kevin addressed Reilly, handing over glossy printouts of the man next to the trashcan and also the closeup of the gloves.

"This is a big help, thank you." Reilly added to the girls, "You two, please stay out of trouble. And thanks."

Chapter Nineteen

"Hey, are you okay?"

"Sure, I'm okay," Kallie replied with fake cheerfulness, clanking her fork on the plate as she clumsily set it down, and then immediately picking it back up for another bite.

"I can tell you're okay by the size of that pie, you know," Tess replied with a sarcastic eye roll. "Everyone who's just fine eats a six-pound slice of pie for breakfast."

"I'm not okay, Tess," Kallie sighed. Their whole section of the restaurant was deserted, but she spoke quietly anyway. "This is crazy. I'm not sure if I can handle it much longer."

"It's almost over, sweetie. Even if they don't find the killer, they have to let us off the ship when we get back to Tampa."

"And what if we don't live that long?" Kallie whispered.

"The only thing that's going to kill you on this ship is that pie. I promise."

"Peanut butter and chocolate cream pie *and* a serial killer," Kallie whined.

"That serial killer is going to have to get through me to kill you. And I'm not leaving your side."

Tess weighed all of a hundred and ten pounds, but she was fierce. Kallie felt better immediately and hugged her best friend.

"If you want to stay locked in our suite and order room service for the rest of the trip, I'll stay with you. But I know you'd rather solve this."

"I really want to," she whined. "But safely."

"Wait, what? When did *you* become the voice of reason? *Safely?* That can't be right." Tess shook her head in mock delirium, and then grabbed a rolled-up packet of cutlery from the next table and removed the fork. "May I?"

"Of course! I can't eat all six pounds of this thing myself."

Stabbing a bite of the decadent pie, Tess continued, "It can't be that difficult to solve. There are cameras everywhere, and he wasn't filmed jumping overboard. And security has searched every inch of the ship, so he can't be hiding."

"Or she," Kallie added.

"So he, or she, must be on the ship. In plain sight. That's a limited number of people."

"A *big* limited number."

"True, but if it's a random psycho, just cruising for the chance to kill complete strangers, we'll never figure it out. So let's just ignore that possibility and presume it's someone who knows one or both of the victims."

"We're going to need more pie."

* * * * *

They weren't expecting to see Officer Reilly again, but he arrived that evening with a knock on their suite door.

"Are we in trouble?" Kallie shouted to him, without opening the door.

"No, not this time."

She opened the door and let him in, and he took his now-usual spot on the barstool. "We did a background check on the guy in your photo. His name is Peter Gri—"

"You can do a background check?" Kallie interrupted. "All the way out here in the middle of the ocean? Don't you need special permission for something like that?"

"We *have* special permission, Miss Brooks," Reilly answered, sounding a little annoyed. "And, I might add, we did a background check on both of *you*, after our first conversation."

"What? Did you find—"

"Oh yes, we know all about the murder in your

hometown. And if you didn't have a perfect alibi for the time of Devin's murder – laughing it up with your friends, in the restaurant, in front of a hundred other people – you'd have spent some time in the brig, too. Three dead bodies in your wake, in less than a year, is pretty suspicious."

Kallie blushed self-consciously, wishing she could disappear – leaving Tess to politely encourage Reilly to continue. "You were saying, Officer Reilly? About the guy with the gloves?"

"His name is Peter Grisham, and he's bounced from state to state since his teens," he stated. "He's currently living in the Orlando area, but he has a long history of low-level crime – petty theft, assault, burglary, fraud, minor drug offenses – which recently escalated. He just got out of prison for manslaughter, after only four years."

"Are you going to arrest him?"

"We don't have any cause yet, Miss Brooks. He duly served his assigned prison time, and digging in the trash isn't a crime – except against good taste."

Kallie sagged back against her seat in disappointment.

"But I have a bad feeling about this guy too," Reilly grudgingly agreed. "It's nothing I can pinpoint in his past, or on his criminal record, it's just a gut feeling. That's why I'm here."

"You want our help?" Kallie asked, sounding

hopeful.

"I know you've been observing him, and his interaction with the Devin family. And while I can't condone that, and it worries me, frankly – I wondered if you remember anything else he said or did? Is his association with Helen Masters romantic?"

"Samantha accused them of canoodling," Kallie mumbled, still feeling embarrassed and anxious.

Reilly smiled for the first time, "Canoodling. I see."

"Helen said it wasn't romantic, though," Tess added. "And we know she's married."

"Her husband gets seasick, as you informed me," Reilly added with a smirk. "So that's why he didn't come along?"

"That's what Helen said."

"Okay, I know some couples vacation separately, especially if they both have high-pressure jobs." Reilly jotted something in his notebook. "It makes sense that he would choose to stay at home if he was going to be nauseated for the whole trip."

"Does that happen often?" Tess asked.

"Oh, we have people spend two or three days in the doctor's office, after they get so dehydrated from seasickness that they need to be on an IV."

"That sounds like an awful way to spend your time off."

"It's usually people who've never been to sea before, and don't know they're prone to it. We've even had people pay to fly straight home from Cozumel. Most of them don't ever try it again," he concluded. "Anyway, you don't know anything else about Peter Grisham?"

"We didn't even know his name," Kallie shrugged.

"Well, it's a little suspicious that a stranger would be cozying up to the travel partner of someone who was subsequently murdered – but at this point it sounds like a coincidence."

"But what about the photograph, and the gloves?"

"We already discussed this, Miss Brooks. He was probably just picking up someone else's litter. Many travelers with long acrylic nails use disposable gloves to apply self-tanning lotions, or even sunscreen. We see them discarded everywhere— on the deck, in the hallways, even caught in the swimming pool filters – and rarely in the public trash cans."

"Does he look like the type of guy who picks up litter?" Kallie asked, sarcastically.

Reilly smiled ironically. "No, Miss Brooks. He doesn't. But we can't always judge a serial killing book by its cover, can we?"

Reilly promised to continue looking at his entire docket of suspects, and ordered the girls to please be careful, yet again, as he put his notepad and pen back in his vest pockets.

"We're going to keep an eye on him, don't worry," he insisted. "But we have other suspects too. Maybe even a few that you two haven't stalked yet."

"We understand, Officer Reilly," Tess replied, giving Kallie a look to quiet her disappointment. "Thank you for talking with us."

* * * * *

"I don't feel like going to dinner," Kallie said forlornly, after Reilly left their room.

"Are you sure? We might get a lecture on seawater mammals and their weird habits."

"I'm too nervous to focus on makeup and heels right now. And I hate that he doesn't believe us. Let's just order room service."

"Okay, you got it." Tess tossed the room service menu across to Kallie. "The chlorine and salt are killing my hair. If we're not going to the dining room, then I'm going to wash and deep condition it – before I look like a scarecrow. You pick something and order for us."

Kallie nodded and started checking the menu, as Tess grabbed one of the fluffy robes and closed herself in the luxurious bathroom.

Not pizza. Not buffalo wings. Not nachos. We need real food, not snacking. Hmm, we already had the fondue.

She picked up the phone and dialed room service. "Hi, this is Kalliope Brooks in room 528. We'd like a double order of shrimp fajitas, please. With extra green peppers. And a side order of guacamole and chips, and two diet cokes."

She thanked them and hung up, then changed into yoga pants and a t-shirt and went outside to sit on the moonlit balcony until the food arrived.

If Reilly doesn't believe it's the 'Babe' guy, then who's left? Laura's creepy date is in the clear. The would-be killer with a grudge has an alibi. The widow was getting sundaes with her kid. Who else is there? Think, Kalliope.

Maybe the would-be killer had an accomplice after all. I should read the letter to the judge again – did he mention anyone other than his wife?

Taking the copies of the letter back out onto the balcony, Kallie pored over them again, looking for a clue she might've missed. She thought until it nearly drove her crazy, or at least until room service arrived and roused her. Then she jumped up and ran back inside, with the letter still clutched in her hand.

Tapping on the bathroom door, she called to Tess that dinner was ready but only heard the shower running. Her best friend must be rinsing the conditioner out, which would only take a few more minutes.

Absently opening the door to let the room service girl in with her cart, Kallie stepped aside – still reading the letter, certain there was something she'd missed.

Did they have a business partner in the toy company? Wasn't there something about his wife having a brother?

Even preoccupied with her latest sleuthing, she breathed deeply of the delicious-smelling fajitas and caramelized onions and peppers. The cast iron skillet was still sizzling merrily on its wooden trivet, and her stomach growled in appreciation.

"Oh my gosh, that smells so good," she sighed distractedly, still reading, as she waited for the delivery slip to sign. "Thank you so much."

Nope, nothing about a brother. Who else could it be?

The door to the hallway swung shut behind her.

"I really can't believe you had to make a mess of this whole thing," the room service girl complained quietly. For a second, Kallie thought she must be talking to someone on a Bluetooth phone. And then the woman turned toward her.

"Wait. Why are *you*—?"

"We had it so perfectly planned," Helen Masters hissed at her. "No muss, no fuss. Samantha's lousy, cheating, lecherous husband dies quietly, and my hired killer hops onto a passing rowboat and disappears into

286

the sunset. But you just couldn't let it go."

Kallie opened and closed her mouth a few times, in shock, trying to reply to the widow's kind and generous best friend – who had suddenly turned into a killer.

How did I not see this?

"Hired—?" Kallie stammered out loud.

"It wasn't even complicated. You really *can* buy anything on the internet these days, it turns out," she laughed, darkly. "But I couldn't convince him to kill you too."

Kallie searched for an escape route, trapped against the door, as the strange woman pulled out a steak knife from the room service cart and moved toward her.

"He killed Bill?" she choked out, absurdly.

"Poor Bill," Helen cooed sarcastically. "He walked in on us talking about the money. And he had to go."

The distance between them was disappearing quickly, and the knife looked bigger and closer each second.

Out of the corner of her eye, Kallie saw the bathroom door open a crack, and thought, "*Stay in there, Tess. Please stay in there, where it's safe.*"

Then the nearness of the crazy woman, approaching her, drew her eyes away.

"Why me? What did I do?" Kallie whispered.

"Pete saw you pick up the room key in the downstairs hallway, before he could go back down there to get it. And then you couldn't stay away from that stupid old, retired cop for ten seconds," Helen explained, and then rolled her eyes. She held the huge knife closer, making little stabs toward Kallie's face to accentuate her words. "I mean, if you're going to be a nosy pest, could you at least be a *tiny* bit subtle?"

"We didn't even know—"

"We can't risk them finding another body on the ship," Helen interrupted her, impatiently. She added with a grotesque leer, "It's so handy that you have these nice big *balconies*."

Kallie felt the room start spinning again. Fighting her panic, she looked for some kind of weapon.

Grab something, Kalliope. Anything, to block the knife. How did this happen? We never suspected her – not even for a second.

But before Kallie could even react, Tess suddenly ran forward in a crouch, smashing the crazy woman in the head with the full, still-scalding cast iron tray of shrimp fajitas. Screaming like an avenging eagle, the tiny brunette warrior knelt over the much taller, armed woman and pressed the sizzling metal against the side of Helen's face to hold her down. The would-be killer screamed in agony and dropped the knife.

Kallie lurched away from them, stumbling in

shock, and kicked the knife aside. Grabbing a pair of stockings from the dresser, she quickly used them to tie up the assailant's hands and feet. Slumping to her knees in exhaustion and staring at her best friend over the back of her attacker – with wet hair streaming down over a face full of baby blue cleansing mask – it was all she could do not to laugh hysterically.

No sooner had she started to relax, though, when the door began to open again. With the last of her strength, Kallie staggered to her feet and charged forward, slamming her shoulder against the door, catching Peter's hand in the opening. He shouted in pain until she let him pull it free, and then she slammed the door shut and locked it.

Tess was already on the phone, explaining to Reilly that they'd been right about Pete and his sneaky trashcan diving, after all – just not *remotely* in the way they'd expected.

Chapter Twenty

"Didn't I ask you *nicely*, to stay out of trouble?" Officer Reilly asked, gathering ice from the freezer for Kallie's injured shoulder. "About a hundred times?"

He carried the small trash bag full of ice, wrapped in a plush cruise line towel, back to the couch and handed it to Kallie, before sitting down on his usual barstool.

"I mean, we tried," Kallie said simply, with a shrug, and then grimaced at the pain in her shoulder.

"The doctor will be here in a few minutes, Miss Brooks. Try not to injure anything else before she gets here."

"Honestly, my pride hurts more than my shoulder," Kallie sighed. "We never even considered her—"

"Not even for a second," Tess added, shaking her head.

"Who would do that to her best friend?" Kallie asked with a frown. "Convince her to get a divorce or something, for heaven's sake. Hire a private detective to catch her husband in the act. But don't traumatize her for the rest of her life! And poor Skylar."

"Ugh, poor Skylar," Tess repeated, miserably.

"She doesn't even feel bad about it," Officer Reilly told them, shaking his head. "When Agent Paul questioned her, she said Devin continued sleeping around for years after the original incident that Samantha discovered. Even after Sam threatened to divorce him and take full custody of Skylar – who, by all accounts, he really did adore – he wouldn't stop."

Tess screwed up her face in an expression of distaste, but Kallie knew she didn't believe the killing was justified.

"Helen said that he even tried to seduce *her,* multiple times. I think her breaking point was when she had to hit him with a shovel to get away, when he trapped her in the garage during a dinner party."

"Eww, his wife's best friend?" Kallie asked, shocked and disgusted.

"Okay, yeah. I would've killed him too," Tess shrugged agreeably.

"Please don't even joke, Miss Russo," Reilly replied, but he smiled. "Our IT department checked out his laptop and verified that he was in a video call with his mistress in Florida that evening, before he was murdered. Not with his partners at the law firm, as he told his wife."

Tess and Kallie both sneered but let him continue.

"And Helen said she saw him with another woman, here on the ship. Getting up close and personal in one of the dance clubs."

"Wait, you mean on the *first day*?" Kallie gasped.

"Wow, that's..." Tess cringed. "He didn't waste any time, did he?"

"She documented it all on her computer, obsessively, in excruciating detail, over a period of years – and she insisted that it justified the murder, as far as she was concerned. She was utterly convinced that she was helping Samantha." Reilly shook his head again, dazed. "But I doubt a jury will see it that way."

"Yeah, that's unhinged. She should've just testified at the divorce," Kallie replied, baffled.

"With as much evidence as Helen apparently had against him, he probably would've given Samantha everything she wanted, just to save his professional reputation. I mean, who's going to hire a lawyer that's so clearly lacking in even the most *basic* discretion?" Tess added.

Reilly nodded. "Such a waste. I don't think 'unhinged' is a clinical term, but it's appropriate. She said she was completely shocked that Samantha was even crying – thinking she'd be relieved, or even overjoyed, to be rid of him."

Kallie sat silently, shaking her head.

"From the way she was talking, I wouldn't be

surprised if we find out that she tried to kill Devin herself, before she located Pete online," Reilly added. "I need to ask the Orlando police if Devin had any suspicious car accidents or hospitalizations in the past year or two. We don't have access to that information."

"What about Pete? What did he say?" Kallie asked.

"Not much of a revelation there. Helen put out subtle feelers on social media, and he sent her a price. Easy as pie."

"Wow. That's terrifying."

"It gets worse. He only charged her five grand. She gave him an extra thousand after he killed Bill, but that second murder wasn't her idea. Bill stumbled on them talking about Devin, while he was looking for a place to sleep."

"Poor Bill," Tess sighed.

"The first murder wasn't poison, by the way," he added. "Not really. Pete didn't try smuggling arsenic or cyanide or anything onto the ship. He just brought the syringe and trusted that he'd find something toxic when he needed it."

"Are you *kidding*?" Kallie asked, shocked.

"Yeah, Pete Grisham's really not the sharpest knife in the drawer. But for an amateur, he got the job done. He said he just swiped some random cleaning product from an unlocked supply cabinet."

"Ugh, death by disinfectant? That sounds horrible," Tess cringed. "No wonder Devin was spread all over that huge buffet table – it must've been agony."

"And Pete had the sense to not throw away the surgical gloves in his own room, where they would certainly have been noticed and collected for testing when we interviewed him. But then he threw them away right out in the public view." Reilly shook his head.

"But even then, he only got caught because he happened to be in the background of our photo," Kallie noted.

"The luck of the devil, as they say," Reilly agreed. "They weren't even on our radar. And with those stolen room service uniforms and IDs, they slipped right past our guard."

"So what happens now?" Kallie asked. "Agent Paul flies them back to Florida on the helicopter?"

"The ship's already headed back to Tampa, so he'll just keep them locked up until we get there. Budget cutbacks, you know. It's expensive to fly that thing."

"At least they'll both end up in jail, right? Even if she didn't do the actual killing?" Kallie asked, sounding hopeful.

"In my experience, in a gun-for-hire case – poison-for-hire, technically, in this instance – the person who does the hiring usually gets a stiffer sentence than the actual killer. Even if Helen's hands were technically clean, she'll likely do more prison time than Pete."

"Music to our ears," Kallie replied with a relieved look at Tess.

Chapter Twenty-One

"I can't believe we're finally getting off this ship," Kallie exhaled, grabbing the railing clumsily as her sea-adjusted legs buckled a little. She grabbed Tess's arm a moment later, catching her as she also stumbled.

They both staggered for a few steps and laughed. Everyone else disembarking from the ship was getting their land legs back too, so they weren't the only ones walking slowly and strangely.

"I'm glad to be on land again, but I don't want to kiss the dirt – with my teeth," Tess added, catching her balance.

"What a waste. We finally got to go on a real vacation, and we never even got to see Cozumel, Jamaica, or Grand Cayman."

"At least we'll have a good story. The radio station will probably want to interview us about it."

"They can have an interview if they give us another free trip somewhere," Kallie suggested hopefully.

"I just got a text from Winchester, and he's

insisting on buying us a night at the Don Cesar," Tess announced with shock, holding up her phone with the message from her boss. The luxurious old pink hotel in St. Petersburg was a famous local landmark. "We may have been pampered on the ship, but I think the stress level eliminates it as an actual vacation."

"That's way too expensive, Tess," Kallie replied quickly.

"Maybe so. But he heard the story on the local news and feels awful for us. He can probably put it on his expense account, anyway."

"Only if he insists, then," Kallie replied with a laugh. "Do you think they take dogs?"

"I actually think they *do* allow dogs. I know Sherman will be glued to you for a month, so they'll have to take him, like it or not."

They walked through the disembarkation area and watched people wave goodbye to each other. So many people, who would never normally have become friends, now exchanged phone numbers and email addresses to stay in touch. Kallie and Tess waved goodbye to many of their charming dinner tablemates, as they searched for their closest friends in the crowd.

"There's Jannie and her friends." Kallie pointed out the small group of women as they walked toward the parking lot. "I'm glad to see she's okay."

"I may have mocked their convoluted logic," Tess acquiesced, looking at the tall brunette, "but she was the only other person who was totally convinced that Devin was dead. She deserves credit for that."

"And there goes Gary, talking to that pretty girl in the green dress. Should we go rescue her?" Kallie asked, adding a moment later, "Oh, thank goodness – it looks like her boyfriend has it covered."

"I love seeing everyone chatting out here," Tess said with a smile. "There's Freddy the fish trivia guy, with his wife. They're so cute."

"There's the knife thief, too. Who would've guessed that he'd save his marriage by stuffing a bread knife down his pants?" Kallie grinned at the couple, who were walking cozily together, holding hands. "We need to get Missy and Laura's phone numbers before we leave. I wonder where they are?"

"There's your dad," Tess cheered, waving across the crowd. "Hi, Mister B!"

They made their way over to Benny Brooks, and Kallie gave him a huge hug – not realizing until that moment how much she'd missed him.

"Thank you for coming to get us, Dad! We could've taken a cab."

"I don't like you taking cabs, kiddo. Besides, it's not that far."

"Thanks for rescuing us, Mister B!" Tess called, running over to hug him too. "We're all still stumbling around like toddlers."

"Well, drag your bags over here and I'll put them on the cart. That'll be one less thing for you to worry about. Please, no murders between here and the car, though, if you can manage it."

"I'm not sure, Mister B," Tess replied, hesitantly. "They seem to be our new favorite hobby."

"When the reporters said on the news that there had been a murder on a Caribbean cruise, I didn't even have to wait for the name of the ship," he told Tess with a smile.

Kallie laughed, though she knew her dad wouldn't have thought it was funny at the time. He was probably even more stressed out than she had been.

She hugged him again, then finally spotted Missy and Laura, and excitedly waved them over.

"These are our new friends, Dad. They even helped the officers figure out the murderer, when they pointed him out in our photo." She introduced Missy and Laura to her father.

"Nice to meet you both. My Kallie sure can pick people to help her get into trouble!" he added with a laugh. "Can I give you girls a lift somewhere?"

"We're taking the shuttle to the airport to catch our flight home," Missy answered. "Thank you so much for the offer – Kallie told us all about you. I wish we had time to stay for a while."

"They live in Georgia, and they're desperate to get home to the cold weather."

"Well maybe we can catch up with you next time we're headed north, then," Benny suggested. "We still drive up to visit my family in New York."

"That'll be perfect!" They hugged Kallie and Tess goodbye, exchanged numbers quickly, and promised to call when they got home that night, then ran for their shuttle.

After piling up the remaining luggage on the cart and hauling it back to Benny's car, a classic Volkswagen Beetle, the girls collapsed in the back seat, more exhausted than when they'd left for their trip.

I know I should be relieved that we're all safe, but I really need another vacation now, Kallie thought to herself.

Before he started the car, though, Kallie's dad took a moment to check his phone, and then typed a quick message. A minute or two later, the phone dinged quietly. He smiled at the response and put the phone away.

"Who are you texting, Dad? Letting Anna know we're back?"

"If you must know, I promised your detective friend that I'd tell him when I saw you. He was following the story on the police grapevine, and I think he was a little worried about you."

* * * * *

The warm Florida sun felt almost like a real vacation, as Kallie met Morrison at their usual outdoor café for breakfast the next day. She'd had a chance to rest and cuddle with Sherman, decompress slightly from the excitement of the murder, and she was finally ready to talk with her detective friend.

Kallie happily ordered a Cuban sandwich, with extra pickles, instead of her regular blueberry pancakes, since she'd waited so long for it. The café didn't usually fix the decadent sandwich in the morning, but the press was already heated up for breakfast – and they were regulars – so they made an exception.

"That's some breakfast," Morrison noted, as she picked up the first diagonally-sliced half of the sandwich.

"Wanna bite?" Kallie mumbled through the first crunchy mouthful of the premier local Cuban bread. "It's amazing."

"Actually, it does look good." He chopped a chunk off the other half, politely, with a knife and fork. "Wow. You're right, that *is* amazing."

"Extra pickles," Kallie added with a smile.

"I talked to Officer Reilly this morning," Morrison changed the subject swiftly, not making eye contact with Kallie. "He said you were really brave."

"You called him on the ship?"

"Mmm-hmm," her friend replied, still focused on his usual bacon, potatoes, and toast.

"Were you worried about us?" Kallie asked with a curious head tilt.

"Kallie—" Morrison looked at her and sighed, then went back to spreading orange marmalade on his toast.

After a minute or two, Kallie asked quietly, "What else did Reilly say?"

"He said you got into a lot of trouble, which doesn't surprise me in the slightest. I told him I was *familiar* with that aspect of your personality," he chuckled. "But he also said you were helpful. And smart."

"That's nice of him," Kallie replied, taking another bite of her sandwich.

"I think he's going to try to get a commendation of some kind, for you and Tess."

"Could he get us another cruise, instead?" Kallie replied with a laugh. "We had to stay on the ship the whole time, and I didn't even get to go snorkeling in Cozumel," she added with a pout.

"You snorkel?" Morrison asked, surprised.

"Well, no," Kallie blushed. "But I wanted to learn. We signed up for the excursion just so I could try it."

"But you were stuck on board the whole time

because of the murder?" Morrison asked. "That stinks."

Kallie looked at him, expecting to see a sarcastic smile, thinking he was teasing her – but he wasn't.

"I'll take you and Tess out snorkeling at Egmont Key next weekend, if you want." He didn't look up from his plate of home fries, and she wondered if he was joking again.

"What?"

"I mean, it's no Cozumel, I'm sure," Morrison added, a little awkwardly, sounding almost apologetic. "But there are sometimes manatees and even sea turtles. And there are cool old underwater ruins of a fort from the 1800s."

"Are you kidding me?" Kallie gawked. "You *snorkel* too?"

"Well, I have a pretty stressful job," he shrugged. "And it's peaceful down there."

"You never cease to surprise me, Morrison. And I think I can safely speak for Tess when I say – we would both *love* to go!"

"Great," he nodded with a grin. "I'll call you both with the details later this week – we can meet in Gulfport. And seriously, I'm glad you're okay, Kalliope Brooks."

* * * * *

Books by Tanya Westlake:

Bloody Mary, Bloody Murder
Piña Colada Calamity
Mai Tai Malice

www.ingramcontent.com/pod-product-compliance
Lightning Source LLC
Chambersburg PA
CBHW070918260626
47162CB00007B/2716